THE LE

SERIES TITLES

Gridlock
Brett Biebel

The Machine We Trust
Tim Conrad

Salt Folk
Ryan Habermeyer

The Commission of Inquiry
Patrick Nevins

Maximum Speed
Kevin Clouther

Reach Her in This Light
Jane Curtis

The Spirit in My Shoes
John Michael Cummings

The Effects of Urban Renewal on Mid-Century America and Other Crime Stories
Jeff Esterholm

What Makes You Think You're Supposed to Feel Better
Jody Hobbs Hesler

Fugitive Daydreams
Leah McCormack

Hoist House: A Novella & Stories
Jenny Robertson

Finding the Bones: Stories & A Novella
Nikki Kallio

Self-Defense
Corey Mertes

Where Are Your People From?
James B. De Monte

Sometimes Creek
Steve Fox

The Plagues
Joe Baumann

The Clayfields
Elise Gregory

Kind of Blue
Christopher Chambers

Evangelina Everyday
Dawn Burns

Township
Jamie Lyn Smith

Responsible Adults
Patricia Ann McNair

Great Escapes from Detroit
Joseph O'Malley

Nothing to Lose
Kim Suhr

The Appointed Hour
Susanne Davis

"*Gridlock* is a beautiful collection of delicious stories that lead one right into the next. Starting with the first set of stories about a traffic jam on a highway, cars backed up and the theories of what caused it, what will end it, what will happen to the abandoned cars. A riveting group to settle you into this journey of surreal, spec fiction, philosophy, everyday people doing not-so-everyday things, and small town folklore. Themes of obsession and exploration of identity, moments of reflection about human nature are combined with wit, satire, and a strong emotional pull. Beautifully crafted, these stories will invite you, no, tell you to read and re-read them as you get to know the wonderful landscape Brett Biebel has created. Very highly recommended."

—Francine Witte
author of *Just Outside the Tunnel of Love*

"In *Gridlock*, Biebel gives us the truest of Americana minutia with traffic jams and heart attacks and Spam, and then he brilliantly juxtaposes it with this sort of frenzied surreal whimsy, until we don't know which is which, and yet what we are left with is a renewed love of small town America and a deeper understanding of what it is that connects us all."

—Eric Scot Tryon
founder and editor-in-chief of *Flash Frog*

GRIDLOCK

STORIES

BRETT BIEBEL

CORNERSTONE PRESS
UNIVERSITY OF WISCONSIN-STEVENS POINT

Cornerstone Press, Stevens Point, Wisconsin 54481
Copyright © 2024 Brett Biebel
www.uwsp.edu/cornerstone

Printed in the United States of America by
Point Print and Design Studio, Stevens Point, Wisconsin

Library of Congress Control Number: 2024930284
ISBN: 978-1-960329-21-9

Cornerstone Press titles are produced in courses and internships offered by the
Department of English at the University of Wisconsin–Stevens Point.

For St. Peter, St. Paul,
and second-fiddle cities everywhere.

CONTENTS

G.

Gridlock 3

Meet Cutes 6

'96 Civic 9

Gridlock II 11

A Fuller Explanation as to This Particular
Incident's Cause 14

A Proposed Solution 17

Word Problem 21

Infrastructure Week 25

R.

Suds n' Such 31

Lightweight 32

Moon Over Moorhead 33

Thirdhand Man 35

The Boy Martyr 36

One Night Only 38

Deli Sliced Right 40

Judith, in the Biblical Sense 43

I.

Redistricting 47

Supreme Court Shortlist 49

Redemption Incorporated 52

Cable News Kafka 55

A Model Approach 57

Affidavit   61
Model UN   63
Red States   66

D.

Asking Price   69
Imitation Cheddar   71
Export Business   73
People, At Heart   76
Scarecrow Jo   79
Night House   81
Wind in the Wires   84
Spam Factory   86

L.

Paul Bunyan Deluxe   91
A Better Mousetrap   92
Clean-Up Crew   94
Fur Trade Days   96
Las Vacas   97
State of Nature   99
Year of the Lizard   102
In the Offing   104

O.

El Bético Auténtico   109
Fair Trade Value   111
All Dressed Up   113
Plexiglass Menagerie   115
Eye of the Storm   117

Power Forward Christ   120
Stadium Seating   121
National Pastime   123

C.

Brushback   127
Cow Town Carnival   131
Gold Stars   132
Holy War   134
Art Garden   136
Relics   140
Inflation   142
Minnesota Miracle Man   146

K.

Civilians   151
High Noon at the Quarry Target   153
Who Can Turn the World on with Her Smile?   155
Redirect   157
Mall of America   159
The Michiko Kakutani Machine   160
Dynamite   165
New Gopher Prairie   167

Acknowledgments   171

A customer can have a car painted any color he wants as long as it's black.

—Henry Ford

G.

GRIDLOCK

It's some 4th of July afternoon, and I-94's a parking lot from Maple Grove to Fargo, and nobody really understands why (particularly since it's both sides, and cabin traffic's always just one or the other, and who in their right mind has a cabin up that way anyway (not to mention what kind of off-his-nut asshole travels on the holiday itself), and Brainerd, sure, that you'd understand, or, okay, maybe Alexandria even, but it's basically just empty nowhere nothing from Fergus Falls on to the border), and yet, here they all are with the cell phone batteries dying and the cars in park and the A/C fluid playing Chinese fucking water torture with the pavement because nobody's moved for going on six hours. Kids are crying in backseats. Parents are thinking about stealing their diapers. The ice is melted, and the tuna fish sandwiches have already gone half-rancid in the trunk, and you can't even pull onto the shoulder (even if there are stories starting to surface about folks who've tried, deranged genius explorers who somehow found an off-ramp only to realize the way home was more complicated than they thought, and some of them (they say) are gonna make it eventually (and apparently at least one car managed to get off at Exit 156, and word is the driver found St. John's and enough bread and wine to keep him happy for a few years at least, and they say he joined the monastery, and now the car's been stripped or sold or maybe sent around like pieces of the True Cross, and this

3

is what passes for hope in these parts at the moment), and others are just straight doomed to wander the outlet malls or the Red River Valley or wherever else it is they happened to get stuck) on account of there's just about nobody hasn't tried it already, and that means this particular traffic jam isn't even straight lines. It's odd angles. Jutted shapes. If you had a plane you might be able to see these cryptic little clusters that look like Stonehenge or dragons or, hell, maybe the Jolly Green Giant, he's more of a Minnesota River man usually, but these aren't your everyday circumstances, and what they amount to is something that gradually starts to dawn on drivers and families and all one after the other, and the horn blasts and cuss words start to fade, and what takes their place is this strange kind of eerie quiet, and it sounds like nothing. Like death. It's doors slamming and feet on hoods and roofs and windshields and then warm beers and mostly flat Dr. Peppers getting passed around and multiplying like the loaves and the fishes (at least for now, though pretty soon you can bet there'll be rows upon rows of makeshift little roadside stands and booths and maybe a roving bicycle sales force, and they'll be offering price-fixed and very likely polluted tap water for something like 18 bucks a pop), and everyone's staring at the sky and speculating about what exactly is causing this whole thing anyhow (and there's all the usual horror stories involving grisly mangled massive wrecks complete with busted glass and people absolutely certain to be DOA), and some of them have heard rumors about this guy they say is out near Sauk Center or Albany or maybe Barnesville (or else all the way up in Moorhead), and he's got a tricked-out and revitalized Winnebago Chieftain just chock full of enough gasoline to run a generator for months (and that's not even mentioning all the baked beans and potato chips and Grain Belts, nor the actual working fucking toilet). There are bands of teenagers on the hunt for this whole setup right now and as we speak (and, frankly, their parents are glad to be rid of them), and, while all this is being passed from driver to driver and on down the line, a man and his wife have made their way to the median, and both of them are lying there in the ditch (and they're probably fully drunk and definitely half-naked, and you figure it's likely they've been screwing right there in the dirt while also understanding it's possible that it's just way too goddamn hot to do anything other than sit around motionless and pray for some hint of a breeze to hit your skin) and looking straight up, and maybe they're asleep and dreaming, or maybe they can actually hear voices. Broken. Static. Whispered. Words humming all overhead and blended with the mosquitoes, and it's all one big code, these two can tell (and they've found each other's eyes now, and maybe their hands too), but they think they've got a sense of it. A feeling. Like they can grasp some message from all the way up at the front, or, well, maybe it's the back (and could be it's both at once), and what it is is something like "sit back." Or "breathe deep." Or "this is everything you ever wanted, ain't it," the real American experience, and the whole fucking cipher is just hanging right there at the edge and all jagged and painful and prophetic. It's swirling and straining and somehow (they swear) almost about to be cracked.

MEET CUTES

Five, ten, fifteen years later, tens of thousands of couples will claim I-94 as the site of their first date. It'll be one of the exit ramps, usually. Sometimes a patch of median. There'll be this trendy wedding motif where everyone gathers at the spot, and the whole party stands in the grass. They circle the ditch. It's like 90% people from Edina or Eden Prairie or Maple Grove (or else maybe Minnetonka or Orono or Excelsior), and 98% of them weren't even in the (by now) world-famous traffic jam in the first place, but that doesn't stop them from picking some exurban or plain old outstate agrarian spot like Monticello or maybe Albany (as long as it's within easy driving distance of a golf course, or maybe like some type of secret hideaway lake) and saying their vows right there. In the open. Sometimes under the stars. Traffic goes by. Horns are honked (or bags of dogshit and old food scraps and live bait are thrown out windows by locals, and each jurisdiction develops these byzantine systems of competition where a certain number of points are assigned to particular targets, and the bride herself is always worth the most, and if you can provide photographic evidence of her with like banana peels in her hair or puking from the smell of rancid milk (and triple the score for an ugly cry, for a distorted face and visible tears), some local watering hole will let you drink for free for one night or three nights or maybe even all summer), and this gets more common as

these sorts of nuptials happen more regularly (and start to
get viral attention from all kinds of media, social and otherwise), and, ultimately, that's what causes the whole fad to die
off just as suddenly as it started , and pictures will be taken
(and uploaded and liked and shared), and some Best Man
or Maid of Honor will stand up and get all sincere. They'll
talk about love. They'll say they were here too, that 4th of
July, when cars were lined up all the way to Fargo and back,
and they remember the way these two looked at each other.
She was wearing a tank top. He'd taken off his shirt. It wasn't
sexual (at least not entirely), but they found each other, and
they talked for days about family and fishing and lifelong
dreams. They built these little grass sleeping bags you can
find on your centerpiece right there, between the rolls and
the champagne. He maxed out a credit card on peanut butter
sandwiches and $18 bottles of water, and they held hands
and genuinely wished that this honest fucking (which word
the best man/maid of honor will use only for emphasis, and,
even then, only if it's a certain kind of crowd) miracle of a
traffic jam would never end, and one night, it happened, and
they won't say more than that, but it was the First Time,
and it was starry and beautiful and just exactly perfect like
you'd want, and maybe the truth is it was. Maybe it went
just like that. And everyone there will know the answer (or
at least have a viable theory), and some of them (the ones
who pride themselves on their realism and honesty, their
willingness to buck all those Minnesota Nice stereotypes,
or else the ones who are just plain jealous) will sit by the bar
and pound shots and tell their own version, and it usually
involves the backseat of an abandoned car, and things are
getting going, and she asks if he's got a condom, and he
says those are going for triple the price of water, but don't

you worry, baby, because your body understands stress and exhaustion and risk, and all the research says no situation like this is ever likely to lead to pregnancy (and it's all got to do with moon cycles and hormones and a woman's intuition), and she rolls her eyes and grabs him in just the right place, and then it's all a moot point anyway, and, afterward, they don't say shit. He falls asleep, and she understands he's a goddamn moron, and of course she'd be better off with me, but there are unspoken pressures, aren't there? Little cultural guideposts you can't help but follow. But you do me a favor and look at her dancing over there and tell me you don't see it. Tell me that's not the look of just hungry fucking desire, and all I know for sure is I'd rather be the first affair than the first husband, and, by this point, the claim is made to an empty glass. A bartender. Couples will be laughing and kids will be shouting, and the ones who know their way around a keg will have hit that just right kind of drunk that's both euphoric and maintainable, and these doubters will think, man, do we pity the lot of them. Because imagine the load of bullshit you'd have to really believe.

'96 CIVIC

I woke up to a crash, and it was halfway onto the front lawn. It didn't have an alarm. Manual locks. I rolled over and went back to sleep.

Later, when the sun had nearly melted the frost, I found a note on the windshield. It looked like a woman wrote it. "Sorry," it said, "Let me buy you a drink." There was a phone number and something neat and controlled about the letters, like she was probably tall and brunette and real skinny like a soccer player, or else I guess maybe still in a daze. In that foggy, post-wreck shock.

The tow truck came eventually. It was getting dark. I watched the guy from the window and dialed slow. Took my time. It's amazing to see the real mechanics work. With their greasy hair and broken knuckles. How they're all reckless and self-assured, and the clamps and cables look nearly magic.

"Hello," said someone on the other end, and it was even better than I pictured. Just enough rasp to sound dangerous. A tiny bit wild.

"You hit my car, I think," I said. "Wrote your number on a note."

"I did, did I? And what did I say?"

"'Sorry,' you said. 'Let me buy you a drink.'"

There was nothing but laughter for a few seconds. Low and private, and I just stood there blinking. The tow guy was in the driver's seat, ignition roaring. He gave a silent nod. Probably some kind of meaningful grunt. You could tell he wished he was already gone.

"Listen, you got the wrong number, pal," she said, "And don't you dare call this number ever again."

The line went cold, and then it was just me. Me alone. Nothing but broken glass out the window. Some of it was orange. It sat there waiting to catch the streetlight, and I thought about grabbing a broom or maybe getting ahold of insurance, but then I realized better to not. Better to let it be. Let it all rot in the system and on the pavement, and it could be sharp and neon and singing in shards. In pebbles and half-deaths and little embedded pieces in some stranger's worn-out soles.

GRIDLOCK II

The same conversation is happening multiple times and all along the line.. Pit stops and thirst and wanting a joint so bad you're breathing deep and trying to catch the smell of skunk. It's philosophical. Historical. Sons to fathers and daughters to mothers, and the only constant (aside from the general theme) is generational divide, and what it sounds like is this:

"We should've built rail lines."

"We did. Sea to shining sea."

"I meant high-speed. Electric. And what's with the we anyway since last I checked you aren't Asian and expendable, and you couldn't even set up the model train I got when I was nine."

"Can dry clean my ass off, though."

"Jesus."

"What?"

"You know what."

"And when did everyone get so sensitive all of a sudden, and, you know, maybe just one little 'thank you' would be nice. Seeing as we built all these roads and this car anyway [and maybe there's an interjection here about how 'and you'll never catch me in one of them foreign jobs, no siree'] and managed to hook it up with air conditioning and satellite radio and a built-in DVD player your [other parent/step-parent/caregiver/guardian and] I make sure to keep nice and

11

working and stocked, and that's not even mentioning that little gizmo in your hand there, and did you ever hear of eye contact? Look at me when I'm talking to you, [son/daughter (and, in at least one case, there's a deliberate misgendering, and it makes the recipient want to strangle the driver with their headphones, except the problem is that they're wireless and, thus, well, you can see the issue.)]"

"Oh, I can see you fine. Better than you can see yourself."

"You can't see shit."

"Not with all the smog around here, anyway."

"That's right. I remember now. All your gadgets run on rainbows and hemp, don't they? No coal miners harmed in the making of this product. Charging it, on the other hand, there you might have an issue."

"Okay, well, um, could we…" says a third party, and then she (or, more rarely, he) says there might be some seven-layer bars (or else M&M cookies) still in okay shape somewhere, and what do you say we settle on one of those agree-to-disagree-type conclusions, which is, of course, a reasonable and rational and Midwestern idea, but it elicits no response. There's only a silence that's equal parts resentment and seething generational bitterness and, also (probably), a certain kind of fear. Of self. Of hypocrisy. Of what if everything's already good and fucked, and all that's left is to just sit here and appreciate each other's company with optimism and generosity and big-hearted ego-subordination (to the point that you don't even take credit for said subordination, and you sure as hell don't add it to some karmic balance sheet you've got all locked and loaded and just waiting to deploy at the exact right time, when a reminder of your sacrifice, maybe even your sheer emotional martyrdom, will be the coup de grâce, the Fat Man and Little Boy, the all-time and

all-purpose trump card that establishes your moral superiority henceforth and forevermore because true and authentic
and genuine altruism means not even actually imagining
the sheet at all), and, tell me, has there ever been any kind
of real fun in that?

A FULLER EXPLANATION OF VARIOUS THEORIES REGARDING THE CAUSE OF THIS PARTICULAR INCIDENT

This traffic jam, perhaps you've already figured, it's a haven for conspiracy. Rumors. Hyperlocal (and fleeting in the grand scheme, though it doesn't feel that way to anyone who's been sitting around drumming the steering wheel for days on end) legend. There's one guy who Googled the world record for longest traffic jam and found out it happened in China maybe 10 or 15 years back, and the thing went on for 12 days. He figures maybe this is their revenge. And, probably, back then and somewhere in Inner Mongolia, there were folks blaming the whole thing on Western influence, trade wars, free markets and foreign meddling, and these things tend to move like boomerangs, don't they? They all come back full circle in the end, and this is what the guy argues, anyway, and he's got his adherents, but the trouble with the geopolitical, act-of-war kind of causes is everyone seems to have different enemies, and pretty soon the country of origin is getting changed to Russia or Iran or, honest to God, Canada (and they say that one started as a joke, but then it got picked up because, after all, jokes are dangerous and always playing on our own insecurities, and you can see the phrase "Fuck Canucks" written in condensation on various vehicles that usually tend to be clustered together in the eastbound lanes and almost always far away from any kind of plausible exit), and so the narrative gets fractured and the groups splinter and they all end up looking like fringy fucking freaks, even though it's really a pretty big number that basically believes just exactly the same type of thing, and that number gets even bigger if you count the folks who think it's an inside job. A snarl-up engineered by the Feds (or maybe MnDOT) for unknown purposes, and this time it's the specific nature of these purposes (and just how nefarious they might be) that causes the cracks because some people think it's all to justify some kind of increased transportation tax or toll like they got in that Godawful Illinois (and this is maybe the one point of commonality across every vehicle stuck here idling is that they'll drive from the Twin Cities all the way down to Bloomington and then over to Danville on 74, and they'll do this even if they're headed to South Bend because, well, because Chicago (and here they shudder with the momentary recognition that maybe they've all found themselves in the middle of something way worse, at least temporarily), and no one needs to offer any more explanation than that) or Ohio or what have you, and others (statistically more likely (by a wide margin) to be Black or (by a thinner one) Asian or Hispanic) think it's about giving certain people lung cancer or really deep sun burn, or else it's maybe some sort of test designed to incite a violent response, after which the photographers and camera crews and pretty blond reporters will swoop in from behind prairie grass and pine trees (or maybe emerge from thousands of little roadside ponds and retention pools) and put the biggest and darkest and most aggressive faces on front pages and TV and cellular screens all across the country, and good luck getting any justice at all if that ever happens, and these folks tend to try and meditate. To block out the shouts and the car horns and the roving median preachers who, after about the first day, wander up and down carrying signs made from t-shirts and fast-food napkin stashes they yanked from the glove box, and these signs are emblazoned with their own personal versions of the True Cause, which are disparate and dependent on type and range from the usual Armageddon eschatology to corporate espionage and covert focus groups and test markets.

"Did you ever notice," says one of these self-styled prophets with green eyes that look about as high as any sober individual could ever manage to get, "how all these little bicycle peddlers riding around got iPhones? And them handheld clickers? And you ask me this right here's about as big of a captive audience as anyone could ever hope to get in these broken times, and you check out your phone, man. What's it showing you? Blue Diamond slivered almonds? Fanta? Arby's or Wendy's, and pretty soon we'll all be looking at the same thing and from whoever's ended the fiscal year just barely underwater, and you do some digging and you'll see. Who's down? Who needs a sales boost? You find that, and there's your whole story, and all you got to do is just follow the money, man. That shit'll tell you everything you need to know."

A PROPOSED SOLUTION

In the early hours of the bottleneck (which, in the halls of political power, was referred to variously as a "logjam," a "snarl-up," a "SNAFU" (later decapitalized to avoid calling to mind a certain forbidden word ,though plenty of people had no problem calling the whole thing a "shitshow" or a "clusterfuck" out loud and in public)), a "roadblock," and an "unprecedented crisis" (and, curiously, the word "gridlock" never did get mentioned, save for once in a white paper that argued it should be avoided at all costs given its political connotations (and, therefore, its potential to cast blame in undesirable ways, and even the opposition managed to avoid it, perhaps because of its bipartisan nature, its all-encompassing suggestion of total, system-wide failure)), an assistant to some anonymous USDOT undersecretary typed out a radical proposal for ending the whole thing in "the most efficient way possible," and the idea was twofold.

1) Immediately restrict all motor vehicle activity within one mile on either side of the interstate (from the 94/494 junction in Maple Grove all the way out to Casselton, ND), including all entry points, and stranded cars and trucks could then be escorted off the freeway in long lines and by state and federal and otherwise official emergency vehicles, ala funeral processions, and

2) invoke a (constitutionally dubious) form of eminent domain that could be used to repossess any vehicle

remaining stranded after 48 hours (given that it was clear that at least hundreds of folks had already abandoned their cars to fate), with the owners being given the high-end of fair-market value (according to Kelley Blue Book), on a promissory basis, in exchange for their (implied) consent to the immediate deployment of an army of drivers (and these could be volunteers, people on loan from ride-share companies, government employees, etc.), who would commandeer each abandoned vehicle and drive it off the interstate and into one of several cornfields that would also have to be acquired via eminent domain, and this would all happen car-by-car until the whole road was empty (and the bonus was that these cars could ultimately be put back into the market; they could simply be given to dealerships along the impacted, 200-some mile route (which would create increased supply, reduced prices, and a potentially massive rise in sales volume, something that, given the modalities of the automotive retail industry, would allow for an injection of serious cash into local economies)), at which time commerce could begin to assert itself once again.

This proposal, we should note, was written in haste, and its references (not to mention its legal justifications) were a complete mess, and objections came from all over. First, there was the whole supply-chain issue of ceasing I-94 transit for days. Maybe weeks. And imagine the truckloads of rotten fruit and cattle left in overheated semitrailers, and this was going to be Depression Era shit. Breadlines (that would actually probably be more like meat lines, fresh produce lines, shelves emptied of toilet paper and canned goods and c., and that's not even thinking about the loss of commercial merchandise and the subsequent hits to all sort of stocks, transpo-related and otherwise (all of which, the plan's author argued, was probably going to happen anyway, and this was their only real chance to limit the damage (which, it had to be noted, wasn't just going to be economic, and what about the emotional toll, the human cost, etc., etc.), even if it meant being overly aggressive, even if it meant a politically untenable approach)) in St. Cloud and Fargo, and maybe even as far west as Bismarck, and who knows how many other places in between, and, second, the whole thing smacked of like Chinese or old-school, Soviet-style state-ownership (and, indeed, almost immediately, the plan's critics dubbed it, simply, Leningrad (even though the original writer had called it Operation Fluid Freedom)), and neither of those arguments even touched the clear issues of federalism, and the 10th Amendment (as well as the 5th) was repeatedly mentioned, even though the original writer included a footnote that argued that Minnesota (at least, though who the hell could say about North Dakota) might give permission. Might be so desperate that they'd basically give up sovereignty over a couple of dozen lakes too (and here it's probably worth pointing out that this original writer, he may have been a bit out there in terms of his politics and general mental state (and rumor was that he was definitely sleep-deprived, and also quite possibly high)), which line did not go over particularly well when the whole thing was leaked to the media the next day, and the protestors (or "militias," depending on your POV) immediately went to work. They had American flags. Signs that said "Our Taxes, Our Land," and there was debate about how many there were, and did they constitute a majority (?), and opinion polling seemed to just think the whole thing was like a 47-41 issue, which, taking into consideration the collective MoE (and the number of "What the fuck are you even talking about, man"s), meant that everything was essentially a wash, and the only thing anyone knew for sure was that, whatever these activists called themselves, they definitely weren't silent. Some of them flew drones over the stranded vehicles, drones that dropped copies of the Constitution, and this went on for the whole rest of the 13 days, and it basically made any kind of radical solution impossible. It ended up more a wait-and-see thing. Nothing else to do but sit around in boredom and tears until the market adjusted and cars avoided the whole area on their own and entire companies rerouted traffic and restructured distribution grids, and, years later, when the incident got to be real en vogue as an object of academic study, the scholarly consensus was this: When it came right down to this particular solution, the protestors were right. It was unconstitutional and, depending on how you wanted to slice it, maybe even a violation of that most sacred American Amendment, the 1st (and the argument here was that it all had to do with the ins and outs of "peaceable assembly"), but the thing about that Constitution? It looked an awful lot like the whole fucking problem in the first place.

WORD PROBLEM

A sovereign nation (call it Sovereign Nation U (U_{SN})) presides over 50 member states, one federal district, and five inhabited territories, each of which issues its own, unique license plate to all registered vehicles within its jurisdiction. Individual member entities of U_{SN} have distinct names signified by E_0, E_1, E_2, and so on, with E_0 possessing the largest number of total registered vehicles at 17,765,625. The total number of registered vehicles in every other individual member entity of U_{SN} (E_1 through E_{56}) can be calculated as an approximate geometric series wherein r = .88. Ideally, decimal numbers should be dropped completely (as in, essentially, rounded down), with the resultant integer being used as the basis for the calculation of the next term in the series (though, of course (and as no one should need to be reminded), including the fractional portions of individual terms (that is, viewing the total number of registered vehicles in each individual member entity as parts of a strictly geometric series (even though, technically speaking, decimal numbers would be an impossibility given the particulars of the hypothetical), rather than an approximate one) will not have a substantive impact on the result). Now, assume a second, imaginary, contiguous, geographic landmass (U_{SNi}) that contains all registered vehicles from each member entity of U_{SN}. The vehicles are distributed randomly, such that a vehicle from E_7, just as a for instance, is as likely to appear as a vehicle from E_{39} at any given geographic point in U_{SNi}. Now (finally), assume an individual (call her person "I"). She'll be born in a hospital at the exact contiguous center of U_{SNi} (which, really, being that the country is imaginary, and, therefore, contains no fixed, definable border, wherever she's born could conceivably be conceived to be the center) at 12:01 AM on a January 1st and die at 4:35 AM on a January 1st. She'll live for 87 years (during which time, it is stipulated that the total number of vehicles registered within each individual member entity will remain constant (though you may, if you like, assume that they change owners at regular or irregular intervals, as suits your individual preference)). The year of her birth will be a leap year. At precisely 8:01 AM on her 10th birthday, she'll (all at once and in a flash) develop an eidetic memory as it relates (and *only* insofar as it relates) to recalling license plates attached to vehicles that enter her field of vision. Assume I sleeps for exactly eight hours (from 12:00 AM to 8:00 AM (and please note that she never leaves her own time zone (and, even if she wanted to, she couldn't, seeing as the conditions set by this exercise (conditions I am laying down right now and as we speak) dictate that U_{SNi} contains one (and only one) time zone))) each night. During her 16 waking hours, she sees exactly 15 vehicles each hour, every hour, until the day she dies. It is her desperate wish to see the license plate design of every single individual member entity of U_{SNi} (which fact owes itself to her inability to visit any of E_2, E_{17}, E_{25}, etc. by any means other than her own (eidetic) mind's eye) before her death, which will occur in her sleep (while she dreams of alphanumeric series printed on variously designed and colored backgrounds (a personal favorite of which will be a sort of M.C. Escher knock-off featuring cars bumper-to-bumper in an endlessly long line (and the bumpers themselves will feature their own alphanumeric series (printed on the same traffic jam background (whose individual cars will have alphanumerics on their respective bumpers and so on and so forth))))). What are the odds said desperate wish will be fulfilled? Create a model that attempts to answer this question (and extra credit if it can also answer the following ones: What are the odds she *only* sees license plates from the individual member entities with the ten largest totals in terms of number of registered vehicles? What are the odds she sees every registered vehicle from E_{55}? What are the odds she sees license plates from every individual member entity *except* E_0 (or E1 and so on)? And c. and c. and c.). This is Part One.[1] Your score will be calculated by comparing the underlying code of your model (as well as its interface, its graphics, and can you watch poor old I's face fall and droop or light up in excitement pending the outcome of individual simulations (and do the chosen polygonal representations accurately capture the human desire for simulated authenticity without entering into the uncanny valley), or can you perhaps set the whole thing to real-time and watch, minute-by-minute, plates passing by until her desperate wish gradually merges with your own and the two become so intermingled that you begin to wonder which is more real (or if either even comes close to the real reality at all)) to that of Happy Hunting, a model that was written mostly (and entirely for the purpose of solving this problem) in 2013 and has been continuously vetted, updated, and

---

[1] It should be noted that the parameters of the assignment allow anyone, for any reason, to ignore Part One entirely, submitting no work and choosing, instead, to "roll the dice," as it were, and take their chances with Part Two. Which, for more, see sub (and, also, supra).

debugged by a panel of experts from various departments across campus, including Mathematics, Computer Science, and Data Analytics. For Part Two[2] you should write a brief obituary (or, if preferred, a final congratulatory or condolence-heavy farewell) for I, wherein you (using your original model's calculations) address the fulfillment/non-fulfillment of her thrice-aforementioned desperate wish. Your document will be graded on a curve by a (pretty watered-down, if we're being honest) version of IBM Watson on loan from Rochester, MN, and "educated" on famous eulogies, tributes, open letters to deceased individuals, previously submitted student work, etc. In the event that your submitted obit/letter/essay/etc. makes mention of the incorrect outcome re: I's desperate wish (as determined by pulling a randomly selected simulation from Happy Hunting), you will earn a zero for this portion of the assignment. You may choose how much weight will be given to each individual part, though please permit a final word of caution: anyone attempting to build and distribute (or even just one or the other) a model that performs any kind of optimized analysis regarding ideal weighting ratios for Part One vis à vis Part Two will see it executed. Poorly. And then those poorly executed conclusions will be applied to your own work, with no exceptions and all the way across the board because some things shouldn't be solved. Some things you have to feel in your guts, and this (unfortunately) happens to be one of those very things.

---

[2] Which, of course, can also be skipped entirely (though, it should go without saying, not if Part One also is).

INFRASTRUCTURE WEEK

On some spring midnight, a father will drive his family's 2012 Honda Odyssey to this empty, nowhere spot on I-94 (and it'll be someplace between St. Cloud and Fargo, though exactly where will depend upon the telling) and leave it parked crosswise. It'll bridge the two westbound lanes, and then he'll bike the 12 miles back home. His wife will report the car stolen. By the time it's found, processed, and returned, two more abandoned vehicles will have popped up nearby. A Chevy Equinox, probably, and a Dodge Caravan. The eastbound lanes will be clogged as well, and, soon, it won't just be 94. It'll be 80. 35. 40 and 440 and 610 (and for whatever reason it's always gonna be only interstates), and all of a sudden it's a goddamned fad. A national phenomenon. Traffic will be stalled, choked off at strategic points on the edges of every major city in America, nothing on the security cams, and law enforcement will come up with all sorts of theories about mass delusion or bored car thieves or global networks of terror, and they won't be able to keep up. It'll become this game of asphalt whack-a-mole, and there's no pattern. No connection. The cars will all be older and generally marketed as "family" options (airbags and cargo room and gadgets coming out of the speakers or sometimes down from the ceiling), but otherwise it's this mix of imports and domestics and imports made domestically, and some of them will have

Confederate flags. "Coexist" bumper stickers. WWJD and Calvin pissing on team logos and political faces that run the whole spectrum, and university parking passes will be all mixed in with fuzzy dice and hula girls and truck nuts while every federal agency you can think of runs these software analyses to try and put together some sort of psychological profile, some kind of map of ideological similarity, but it won't matter. Even if they find one. Cars will keep coming, and none of the PSAs will work (and there'll be plenty of research suggesting they're all probably counterproductive), and could be it's protest or maybe something to do with entropy, and there will be whole internet groups devoted to finding non-interstate routes to and from every location imaginable (not to mention a number of wealthy individuals who will set up shadow organizations, entire endowments for the sole purpose of buying cars in order to abandon them (and shell corporations designed to hide the original purchase records and so on)) and a few doomed pieces of legislation proposing something like a return to continental rail, or else escalating and draconian punishments for the owners of anything left unattended within miles of an interstate, and eventually what the authorities will have to do is simply take immediate possession of all these vehicles (and a good chunk of them will then be resold only to end up left on some other highway (or, in a few documented cases, the same exact one)), and there will be no stopping any of it. Part of life. A new normal, and everyone will feel it. Experience it. Convoluted cultural debates will bob to the surface weekly, daily, all the time and constantly, and there will be wide-ranging (and often circuitous) discussions about renegade individualism and the regulatory bureaucracy, transit webs and supply chains and the responsiveness of political institutions and c., and for an entire generation of newly licensed drivers the whole thing will become an emblem of American identity. The American future. A formative vision of the new American truth.

R.

SUDS N' SUCH

The kid would only sleep at the automatic car wash, and that's where we decided on the divorce. He was quiet. Finally. Backseat, drooling away, and we'd started going there together. It was the only time we could talk. The machines were doing the windshield, bristles on glass, and Fern said, "It's not your fault, you know," which was true, of course. Never a fucking doubt.

"It's his," I said.

"Damn right."

"Not like we can blame him, though, is it?" and soap chased water chased dirt all across the glass, and she flipped on the radio and said we could. In a whisper. Almost a threatening sigh. I hear it when I drive back there. In the spray hitting metal and the sound of wet tires, and I like the way it feels at night. When there's no one around. You can close your eyes, and the whole place is some kind of jungle, is Ecuador or, I don't know, maybe Brazil, and it's just waves and rustles and rinse cycles, and the thing of it is it's the whole rest of your life. Everything you own. All polished up and eating some serious goddamn shine.

LIGHTWEIGHT

I was supposed to marry this girl whose brother won a Division III wrestling title, and she took me to see him once, at some big meet up near St. Cloud. He made weight at 133, and, honestly, he didn't look like much. Like a cornstalk, maybe. A ribbon of interstate late at night, and the reflective paint is hitting your face in strips, and he had the first kid he saw on the mat in about 12 seconds and then stared at the two of us up there in the bleachers like we were insects, crepuscular moths or something, and, later, between bouts, I was eating a hot dog, and Melissa was in the bathroom, and he came over to me and started talking about atoms, about how many there were in the human body and how they were all changing all the time and moving all across space, and he said somewhere inside him was this tiny piece of Hannibal Barca's dying breath, and he could channel it at will, he said, and everything felt static for a minute. Palms slapped foam. Bodies collided. Somebody was limping away from his match, and I could feel the bun collapsing in my hand, and now his face looked more like an exam, a word problem or a blue book, and I don't know what I said, but it wasn't anywhere close. It must have been as wrong as anyone can possibly be.

MOON OVER MOORHEAD

Jimmy and I go to this play in Minneapolis, and there's a nude scene, and he can't stop staring at the actor's ass. There's a birthmark on it that looks just like Texas. Like Jesus. Like that Milwaukee Brewers logo with the baseball and the glove, and it all depends on who you ask, and he gets real obsessed about it. Wakes up screaming. He can't figure out if it's real or if it's makeup or what kind of message it's supposed to send, and if it's about character or fame or what it means to even be looking, and so he goes to see the show seven, eight times, and this is a man with zero artistic bones in his body. Can't sing. Can't dance. Thinks anybody who can't change their own oil is a "goddamn pussy," and we were never a good match, but he calls me one night. In winter. It's way past dark. There are two feet of snow in Fargo, and he says he found the guy's old girlfriend, the actor's, and I can tell he's describing her with his hands.

"She looks like you," he says, and they meet up near Highway 75, out by the Red River, and he asks about it. About the guy's ass. I guess she just looks at him. She says she made a drawing once. Pencil and shading, and she still has it somewhere, back at her apartment, and they go over there, and he says he'll give her 500 for it. It's probably everything he has. As I'm listening, I'm thinking how it's maybe not the worst thing he's ever spent money on, and there's this pause on the other end. It's like you can feel magnets in the background. Garbage trucks.

"Well," I say. "What's the verdict?" But he just grunts, and then the line goes dead, and it's about two weeks later the package shows up. The corner's ripped. I unroll it, and I wonder if it's an original or a copy or some sick joke on account of how I once told him he'd probably end up divorced and happy and watching football alone in his basement, and the picture's all gray and smells like cigarettes, and you can't even see anything, really. It's light like a paper airplane. It feels like a boat that's been sent out to sea.

THIRDHAND MAN

At Stenie's, we played cards until three, and I had five beers and lost $86. The weather was getting warmer. I put the windows down on the drive home, and it always feels nice to let some snowmelt into your lungs, and Celeste wasn't worried, but I called her anyway. It barely rang. Sent me straight to voicemail, which, I figured. Typical.

"I always hated your mother," I said to the machine, knowing I couldn't take it back, and the truth is that was fine by me on account of we both remembered that time at her uncle's place up in Brainerd, and I was late because it was 2-for-1s at McBleacher's, and we were on a pull tab hot streak, and when I got to the cabin, her mother said I smelled like a pool hall or one of them discount motels off of Route 10 and had to drape the whole chair in a garbage bag before I could sit down. "Ma'am, I ain't never smoked in my life," I said, but she told me it didn't matter. That shit travels. "You'll poison us all just the same."

THE BOY MARTYR

I'd had sex before I met Davey, but not much, and it was mostly unsatisfying. With guys who were real earnest. Too earnest, probably. Like you could tell they prided themselves on respect, but maybe it was all just a pantomime of respect, and they were only doing it so they could talk themselves to sleep at night, defend themselves to current mothers and future daughters and also maybe some deranged version of my dad. Davey was different. This was in college. He played football. Almost good enough to start. He took me down into these tunnels underneath the Abbey, and there were beer cans and Frisbees and candles, and everything smelled like incense. Like Mass at night in late November. We didn't have a flashlight. I kept tripping, and somehow his hands were always in the right place, and I didn't know if it was some athletic balance thing or else maybe just all part of the plan. We came out into some kind of basement chapel, and there was an altar and these little honeycomb niches all along the walls.

"Reliquary," he said.

"Uh-huh."

"There's fingernails in there. Pieces of hair."

"And you thought this would be romantic or…help me out here."

He shrugged. His shoulders made a sound. A pop almost, and it echoed, and for a second I thought there might have been a bat in my hair. "I don't know," he said. "My theology teacher told us there's a skeleton under the altar. Some Greek kid or something. He didn't go to the king's birthday. They whipped his ass with boiling lead."

"Even better."

"You can't see him, but I don't know. I guess I thought maybe you could."

I can't explain it, but something made me put my hands over his eyes. We took a couple steps forward. His arm found my waist. There was pressure on my hip and a finger underneath my shirt. We heard somebody walking around up above our heads, but we didn't pay that much attention. I guess I figured maybe they were looking for us, and maybe they weren't, and what the hell did it matter anyway when we were both of us there. Both of us alive. Both of us picturing silk scarves and orbital bones and the way there's all these places you just really wish you didn't want to look.

ONE NIGHT ONLY

The neighbor had a few trees removed, and they had to leave the trunks out on the lawn overnight. The sun went down, or the truck was full, or else I guess they maybe just needed a break. They were ash trees, I think. Diseased. I called Rachel, and we went over to look at them, and they'd all fallen at some pretty weird angles. One of them was perched on the cut branches of another, and we slid underneath and then just laid there in the dark for a while. We couldn't get our arms around the wood. Every so often, we'd try to push it, and it wouldn't budge, and the ground was slick and wet, and so our bodies made these little outlines in the dirt while we talked about cremation. Like, the virtues of getting turned to smoke versus buried down deep. "There's something about the skeleton," I said, and what I meant was how I couldn't imagine losing even your bones. We were drinking from thermoses filled with coffee and her mother's cheap peppermint schnapps. It tasted like Christmas. Like mint toothpaste gone bad. One of the trees must have had 150 rings, and another had 47, and that was the only one we counted specifically because the rest just seemed like way too much work.

"Jesus Christ," she said, , "it was practically a fucking baby," and I told her how even the oldest one was like maybe our age at the very most. "It's different for trees," I said. "The scale, I mean, and I guess time is relative, and it all depends on like your particular angle in space."

We were both pretty drunk, but I swear the neighbor was watching us through the window. The TV was on. You could see the blue light. Sometimes it would shift to different shades, and from the pattern I figured it must have been a baseball game or maybe a cop show, and it didn't matter because you could feel the guy staring all the same. "He's waiting for us to kiss," I said, and I didn't mean anything by it. It was more like a running joke. I bet she thought I was serious, though. She kind of arched her back and peered toward the window, and, "Fuck him," she said, and I think I probably understood her. Even the stumps would be gone and disappeared gone.

DELI SLICED RIGHT

My girlfriend slept with this guy who worked at the Rainbow Foods on Snelling, and we waited for him in the parking lot. Me and Lyle. He talked me into it. I said, "Shit, I stepped out on her two or three times already, so I figure it's only fair, ain't it," but he said something about honor. The olden days. Bar fights and switchblades, and they tell you the rules are changing, the ones about men and women and sex and desire, but maybe they're not, he said. Maybe they shouldn't be, and so there we were waiting. I didn't know what we were planning exactly, but maybe just scare the guy. Get a good look at him. Anyway, he comes out, and he's 6' 5". Looks like a linebacker. He's carrying about four plastic bags all stuffed with shaved turkey and honey ham and the rest of the cheap shit, and we run up to him, and Lyle goes, "Hey, you know Rachel, don't you?"

"Who's asking?" the guy says, his voice all hoarse from something. A cold, maybe. Or else from talking over the machines.

"This here's her boyfriend," says Lyle, and he looks at me expectant. You gotta remember this is broad daylight now. Three, four o'clock on a Friday, and the lot's starting to fill up, and people are coming in with their kids, and everything's got that end of the day stress hanging on it, and I don't really know what to do, so I wave. I actually fucking wave.

"Hey," says the guy.

"Hey."

"Jesus Christ," says Lyle.

"You know, the thing with Rachel, I don't know if she told you, but we go back. Her brother and me, we used to play ball together, and I think it was one of those old-time nostalgia things, and it's none of my business, but she didn't tell me anything, man. I swear. Not a goddamn word."

"You got anything good there?" I say, "Some of that Boar's Head, maybe?" I'm smelling sodium, and I haven't eaten lunch, and this whole thing was Lyle's idea anyway.

"In back," he says. "Let me. You know what man, hold on. Wait here. Peace offering." He bolts back inside, and we hear the auto doors, and Lyle and me sit on the curb.

"And one of them little whiskey bottles too." Lyle yells, but the guy is already long gone. We don't have any cigarettes, so we just tap our feet and watch moms with too much makeup and people struggling to get on them motorized scooters and these high school kids all dressed like burnouts, and the guy's not coming back. We know this. Or, at least, Lyle thinks he does, and you can tell he's wanting to hit me, or to hit someone anyway, given we made the trip and all, and he says, "You know there's two of us, don't you? And one of him?"

"What about it?"

"Two is more than one, numbnuts, fucking think about it, and do you even love her?"

"Aw, Christ, do you?"

Lyle looks stunned by this. Hurt even.

"Fuck you," he says.

We're deadbeat silent for God knows how long after that, and I'm thinking about this scar Rachel's got underneath her shoulder, and she says it's from a firecracker, 4th of July,

1996, and it looks a little like a star. An explosion out deep in space.

"Whatever. Let's get out of this shithole," Lyle says finally, and, as he does, we see the guy exiting way down by the pharmacy. The whole other end of the store. Lyle is livid. "Pussy," he screams, dragging it out at the top of his lungs, and you can see the guy stop. The whole goddamn parking lot. Everything is in freeze time, and the guy launches one of them deli bags, and we watch it flying. Everyone watches it. It arcs across the lot and over fast-food wrappers and pop bottles and carts and rusted SUVs clocking 100, 200K, and it looks like roast beef. Pink flapping inside plastic, and in an instant, I know me and Lyle are both after it. We're salivating. Our heads are going to collide mid-air, and we'll be hopelessly tangled, and, when we hit the pavement, rocks and broken glass will stick in our skins and scratch up our legs, and we'll be two dogs, really. Tearing into scraps we maybe don't even want.

JUDITH, IN THE BIBLICAL SENSE

After college I lived with three other guys in Minneapolis, and that winter it must have snowed 15 feet, and so we bought one of those sex robots from Japan. Maybe Korea, I don't remember. She was customizable. There was some wrangling about body types and builds, and I think what we decided on was called "Yogic," and she came with several detachable wigs and all the standard outfits. Cheerleader and nurse and the like. One of them was agriculturally themed. Another involved the Old West, etc. The UPS guy delivered her in this nondescript box that looked like it came from IKEA, but he nodded at us through the window. Could have been my imagination. Somehow it seemed like he knew what it meant.

We didn't say much about her after she showed up. Named her Judith. That was about it. We put her in this closet next to the jackets and boots, and there was a kind of like code of silence, I guess. Unspoken rules about usage and cleaning and always putting her back in the exact position you found her so as not to spoil the illusion. The sense that she was yours and yours alone, and maybe the other three didn't even know who or what she was. Never understood she was there. Sometimes, though, you'd go into that closet and brush aside the sleeves, and it would look like her arm was bent at a different angle. Her smile more thin-lipped. Slightly less devious. You never knew if it was some trick of the light or something more serious, and in the end what you did was try to ignore it. All you could do was shrug and go about your day.

When we moved out the next year, we took her apart. Hid the pieces in weird places. Behind the fridge. Under the oven. You get the idea. I got my own place now, but I like to think about her when I go out and shovel snow. The sky is clear, but the streetlights block out the stars, and your breath mixes with exhaust, and it feels like 1987. I wonder if anyone ever found her. If she's still there and waiting to be assembled and then turned on, or if she's scattered and dusty and gone for good. Then, I think of how we all used to feel on Sunday nights, when football was over and 60 Minutes turned everything all quiet and aging and solemn, and I wonder if maybe one of us went back and got her. How, some things, there's just no way anyone can know.

I.

REDISTRICTING

We drew the map in a room on the eighth floor. It belonged to a law firm, I think. There was a view of the lake. Technically, I guess I should say that we didn't do any of the drawing ourselves. It was this other guy that did it. We called him Robot Ron, and maybe the most accurate way to put it is he had this computer that did the work. He'd come in with these massive carboard maps, and they'd be highlighted in red and blue, and he had eyes that always looked closed. Glasses with the double bridge like in the 80's or 90's or something, and we sat around eating donuts and sometimes looking out the window at these coeds on their way to class, and you really couldn't see nothing, so most of it was for show, I guess. Some of us had a couple of pretty involved theories about hairstyles and braiding patterns and what they all said about like personalities and certain kinds of proclivities. But Ron, he never looked. Sometimes he had these easels set up all around the room, and there was zoomed-out views of the whole state and then blown-up diagrams of single districts with names like "The Spider" or "Babar" or "Screaming Eagle," and I remember this one had ███████ cut up into maybe four pieces, and the senator from there, he didn't like it. We kept looking at him and telling him he was crazy, and just what was he thinking arguing with a computer, but he was insistent. Said he didn't care if it meant losing his seat, and he met his wife there, goddammit. They were freshmen in college and had this accounting class together, and one night they both got real drunk and went walking down by the river, and then they snuck up into this old movie theater. Some hipster indie was playing. A western, I think he said, but one of them westerns that's got some point about moral decay or like the physical toll of violence, or maybe it was women or Indians who turned out to be the heroes in the end, and anyhow, he said the place served like beer and pasta, and they drank some more, and he went up her shirt right there in the balcony while gunshots or cellos swelled in the background, and neither of them slept that whole night and maybe for like two days after, and there wasn't no way he was gonna approve any map that didn't put the entire fucking city of ████████ in his district. Too many goddamn memories. Too many corners filled with pioneer ghosts.

The room was silent for a minute after that. Robot Ron got this look like he was processing. Frozen. Does not compute. Then, Senator Blimpke, from ████████, he started laughing hysterically and said something like you'll be about eight years divorced by the time the next census comes up, pal, so maybe you oughta leave the sentiment at the door. Ron pushed his glasses up with his finger and crinkled his nose. I concur, he said. And there is no place for emotion in this particular process. Beep boop beep boop. I looked around the room, and you could tell from the guy's face, he wasn't long for the club, and I think we let him keep the district. Keep ████████. The next day, Ronny Boy had this jagged little circle around it, and it looked like a dying star, or maybe like a porcupine on the verge of combustion, and the college girls kept on walking by down below, and we opened the windows and said dangerous things we knew they'd never hear, and right from then on it was like one less asshole to worry about. One more guy who never understood the rules.

SUPREME COURT SHORTLIST

It always includes this woman from the Ninth Circuit, and they say she lets a computer write her opinions. Nobody knows if that's true. Consensus is probably not, and there was this paper in the Nevada Law Journal a few years back that traced the whole thing to a little telephone confab she had with some reporter out of Anchorage. This was when she was a district judge. Hearing a case way down in Ketchikan. Something to do with fishing rights or copyright on a series of totem pole photographs, and the article says it was all supposed to be on background, but there was a bad connection, and it ended up on a wire. Reuters. AP. Etc. Got picked up by USA Today and a few of the tabloids and had a day or two in the sun before going underground for good, and now it only really shows up in legal circles. Certain DC bars just coming around last call. There's lots of guys who argue the story's the only reason she makes the list, and it's all in line with some kind of circus freak show mentality. The crazy old lady (even though she's actually younger than a lot of them) from Alaska who's got a way with narrative and knows how to capture our modern techno-sci-fi imaginations, and there's all kinds of speculation about how this machine would actually work (and the participants always point out that this is just a hypothetical, a thought exercise, and they drink and laugh and sometimes avert their eyes to hide the fact that maybe they really do believe). The main theory is it's got the whole database of Supreme Court opinions (and it's important to note that they don't even stop to consider (and you can just imagine the fallout if they did) that maybe she's feeding the thing like moral philosophy, training it on John Rawls and Peter Singer and maybe even like Rachel Carson) and is capable of matching amici to the fact patterns of controlling cases, and maybe it even cross-references them with various appeals court decisions (all of which are, of course, readily accessible to anyone with a goddamn library card or university ID) and then runs some kind of linguistic analysis to try and capture the flavor of, say, a Scalia, a pissed-off (which, when isn't he, hahaha) Thomas, a careful (or just blatantly hesitant) Roberts. Then, no, says somebody, and her touchstone would clearly be RBG, or else, okay, maybe O'Connor, and they all agree that this is probably more accurate, but the point remains the same. Because it isn't about talent. It isn't about the law. What it is about is an attempt to turn human rationality and legal brilliance into nothing but math and mechanics, and the good old Chief Justice would call it "sociological gobbledygook," and this is plain enough to everyone. It's real fucking easy to see. And here someone always says he'd love to see her nominated, if only just for the rejection of it. The laughter. The Luddite screeds that would play over and over all day long and assert once and for all the human beauty of human systems and human language (legalistic though it may have to be), and they all drink to this. They smile. They walk out into the Federal night and aim their cars toward the Beltway, and it doesn't hit them until Maryland. Sometimes Virginia. Oncoming headlights and Langley all lit up, and the idea is her little computer? What if it actually tells the truth? Makes arguments. Offers forthright perspectives and legal, and maybe ethical, philosophies and all with a certain linguistic facility. All with a prosaic elegance of which even Scalia could only dream.

REDEMPTION INCORPORATED

There's this outfit out of St. Louis that specializes in apologia. Big-time client list. Celebrities and politicians and public figures, and you know the type. The kind that gets caught up in scandals that get full color photos in everything from the Times to the Post to the Enquirer, and we're not just talking about the usual affairs and teenage sexting, no siree, Bob. It's more like the cheating on the wife while she has late-stage ovarian cancer and with the best friend that always took her to chemo, or maybe flying to Peru on the public's dime to see the mistress you actually think you're in love with, or even picking up a $20 prostitute when you're the King of American Hollywood sort of thing, and the folks that write for this company, man, are they the real fucking deal. You've never seen a group more linguistically gifted and socially aware, and they got this whole thing about how most consulting firms, most political PR teams, what they strive for is like 52% approval. But these St. Louis people, they actually believe (as in it sure don't seem like any kind of advertising stunt) that "real, outright sin is the only thing that ever moves the public needle." That, in order to get really popular, like sanctified popular, Bush post 9/11 popular, you've got to "fall and fall so goddamn hard you become reborn on the way back up," and, no kidding, this shit works. Documented and proven to be effective. They can show you the numbers. It's like they know how to walk the line between real contrition and subtly-blame-others contrition and then full-on defiance, and it all depends on the context, of course, but there's this one story about a woman who was some at-large House member from a nowhere red state, and all of sudden it comes out that she had an abortion at 29 (clearly an age when she was "old enough to know better," according to her primary opponent). St. Louis crafts this real stemwinder for her, this old-school, Great Awakening, tent-fucking-revival thing, and, like all great speeches, it's at once a throwback and a revolution, and she talks about doubt and the devil in this way that makes conservative hearts swell with compassion. Even the hardcore liberals, they don't want to change the channel, and, okay, maybe they're thinking all kinds of biting cynical shit, but the crazy thing is, they're too embarrassed to say it out loud because, at the very least, they know how to read even a televised room (and even Twitter (of all places) is deathly fucking quiet), and now, of course, this woman is a goddamn Senator. Regularly vetted for cabinet positions. Once the Vicepresidency. A quadrennially rumored top-of-the-ticket candidate, and what these St. Louis people do, folks, it's an awful lot like some kind of verbal voodoo, and clients can get in and out real quick, and actually the standing rule is they can't be around when the speech gets crafted. No input allowed. Catch a Cards game or go try and play at the chess club (and that's where most of them do the photo-op), but stay the fuck out of our way, basically. Leave us alone, and do what we tell you, and all these clients, they know better than to put up any kind of resistance there. They go along. Read it word-for-word, and the thing is, as much as these Missouri masterminds should like revel in their ability and flaunt their success, nobody knows who the hell they are.

Not the faintest clue. And all we get are rumors and hearsay, and the only story that's been recorded and substantiated is that they don't even celebrate when an account's closed. The atmosphere post-speech (and along every step of the dramatic (re-)rise) is practically funereal. Nobody knows why. But it's just dead silence, and the client's on a rocket to the moon, and yet everybody who helped draft the statement is commuting all around 170 or 270 (or sometimes 255), and the theory is that they all know that every success brings them closer to some preordained expiration date. Every account (and apparently there's a complicated algorithm constantly working to estimate just how much runway is left) raises cynicism. Hardens the public. Instantiates a kind of bitterly resentful style of reflexive rhetorical criticism, and it's little by little and inconsequential in terms of individual moments, but, in the aggregate, the story's a lot different, and the company motto is something like get it while you can. Because there is a tipping point. And, pretty soon, it's just another American business gone boom and belly-up.

CABLE NEWS KAFKA

One morning, John King awoke to find he'd been transformed into a giant US map. Parts of his body were at war with each other. His armpit (which was somewhere in coastal Maryland) throbbed an angry red. His asshole (near Los Angeles, he thought) felt like a burst blue hemorrhoid. The two were connected. That much was clear. Every so often he understood that he was changing shapes, and one minute he'd be wholly occupied by the Commonwealth of Pennsylvania, or else maybe Wisconsin, and parts of him would be highlighted, Eau Claire and Lackawanna County and the like. After a while, the phone rang. It was probably his producer. King was due at the studio by now. He tried to say he was sick, but it turned out he couldn't move, let alone speak. At the moment, that wasn't a big deal. If they had to bring in a substitute for the day, they could, and television moved fast. He did worry about the implications long-term, though, about whether his carefully cultivated ratings would drift to Spastic Steve Kornacki or Superior Nate Silver, and something became hot and swelled in his chest. Right where Kansas would be. Or Nebraska. Somewhere. Time passed. The phone kept ringing periodically. So did the doorbell. At one point, Dana Bash peered in through the window, and she seemed not to notice, and he tried to flash and spin and toggle and click, but it didn't do any good. She sighed in a way he couldn't actually hear, but of course he knew what it sounded like, and his brain (which felt weirdly removed, like it was hovering above it all, somewhere in Greenland maybe, or possibly Canada) filled in the rest. Like when you have sex in a dream and really experience all the various sensations. Night fell. He could feel owls and raccoons outside, staring at him. They were eating. They were enthralled. Their eyes were fixed, and he found himself strobing. Everything was soundless. Pupils bored in. It must have been an entire village out there, rodents and birds and insects, and they'd gathered on the other side of the glass and decided he held some sort of secret, that he possessed something more important than pain and fear and instinct and mating season, and as he bruised, as his skin became tinted and hued and nearly goddamn purple, he could sense them all searching, failing to grasp what it was.

A MODEL APPROACH

Throughout recent election cycles, various news organizations, consulting groups, Wall Street firms, and c. have published (and regularly updated) a slew of electoral forecast models whose mission is to translate (via a computer simulation approach) a range of possible presidential outcomes (inferred based on polling data, election "fundamentals," historical precedent, demographic trends, news events, etc.) into a visually appealing, easily digestible picture that ultimately reduces itself to a base probability (i.e., "Candidate X will win 86% of the time" or what have you). These models have increasingly become a significant factor in the development of the horse-race media narrative, serving as what basically amounts to a scoreboard, a way of keeping tabs on the big-picture progress of the campaign. Now, the code structures underlying all of these various models are, of course, unique (and often proprietary), but the fundamental process is essentially the same. Input polling data. Control for variables. Use historical datasets and run the simulations, and voila. Achieve a range of potential outcomes and a final probability score.

The great advantage of these models (depending on your perspective, it should go without saying) is their ability to measure uncertainty, to provide broad strokes, to account for the totality of data, so as to avoid getting caught up in the minutiae of every single poll. From a campaign point of view, however, the electoral process is quickly reaching the point where the models (and they do "cluster;" they do tend to agree on the basic contours of the race, even if there are minor discrepancies here and there) dictate the media framing of a particular election to an astonishing degree, and this is potentially problematic because campaigns must respond to the models. They are an exigency in the same way a debate is, or a truck bomb going off in Beirut, or a well-sourced story on a specific candidate's history of extramarital affairs (of liking hot candle wax dripped on her inner thighs, for example, or maybe going out of his way to request call girls who can fit into his high school baseball uniform), and they cannot be controlled. They are unresponsive to spin. They are (or have the appearance of being) mathematical and insulated from the vagaries of rhetoric and campaign advertising and "persuasion," however you want to define it. Fortunately, you do have options at your disposal (because you have to do something, and nobody wants to hear you say shit if you can't at least look like a winner), and the full power of the campaign can indeed be restored because, as it stands, it's hard to run out of money. This is a fact. The stakes of elections are so high (and true believers (of all political stripes (and many with deep pockets))) so rampant) that both major parties have essentially built an ATM infrastructure. Cash is always available, and some of it can be used to flood the polls. What you do is set up shell firms. Buy out whole university political science departments (and if you somehow think this can't be done, then take a look at Hillsdale (or, really, just about any mainstream university on the left)) and thinktanks. You fund survey after survey and poll after poll (and all from differently named research organizations), and then you shift the numbers as far as the methods will bear (and often in opposite directions, okay, because you want it to look right, to look messy and scientific and real), and you move the models. Slowly (and not necessarily even toward you because there is such a thing as complacency and enthusiasm, and you don't want to be losing, but you don't want to be a "sure thing" either), or maybe not at all. Maybe you keep them anchored. It really depends on what you want that final probability to look like, and here's the thing. The other side's going to be doing it too. And there will be a kind of Cold War thing going on. Mutually Assured Destruction. As in, sure, you'd rather spend way less on all of this (and so would they), but the second you do, you know they'll double their inputs and vice versa, and so what's going to happen is you're going to fight them to a truce. You're going to inject money into the economy (the political consulting economy, mostly (which, thank you very much)), and that's never a bad thing of course, and the real major benefit is that all these models end up pretty close to toss-up territory. Or, okay, maybe you get real lucky, real strategic with the timing, or you hire some kind of coding genius, someone who understands methodologies and vulnerabilities and the way the structure can be manipulated (or hell, maybe you're even the charismatic type, the Real Thing, the once-in-a-generation talent that defies our current era of polarization (but probably you shouldn't count on it)), and ride the wave to 70-30 favorite status (and remember there are going to be "independent" (because you should never concede that they're any more "legitimate," any more "real" than anything you're cooking up) polls out there too, and they're going to matter, and the models will learn and adjust, and they'll take your plays (and your opponent's) into account, and maybe they'll manage to distinguish the signal from your tricked-out speakers belching heavy metal noise, but that's probably unlikely, or at least a very long way off), but that's about as high as it'll get. People (who are always hopped up on anxiety and fear and move-to-Canada threats (which, have you ever heard anyone actually make good on one of those?) in any election year) will refresh constantly and hope for reassurance, for some meaningful change in the numbers, but they won't get it, and the bottom line is everything will always be just close enough, and that's the best thing for everyone. For you. For them. For the media and whoever it is that's publishing these models because who the hell sticks around for a blowout, a 98-2 landslide certainty, and then it all just matters that much more. The speeches. The ads. The news. Everything gets tinged with the potential for change, and they're hanging on your (and their) every word, and third-party voters get ostracized as louts and whiners and disaffected, nonstrategic simpletons, and, yeah, okay, you'll spend about a billion per cycle all told (and they might even spend a touch more), but it's better than the alternative. And all in the service of the greater public good.

AFFIDAVIT

The author of this story (which is to say the author, not the narrator or the authorial persona or whatever) met Karl Rove once, at a bar in Bettendorf, IA. This was one of the hazards of living in that particular state. You'd sometimes run into political types, and usually it was at a campaign event, and so there was a feeling of canned orchestration, a manufactured buzz about it all, but sometimes there wasn't. Sometimes it was quiet and intimate and natural, and for a while this made the author feel powerful, like he had some secret influence nobody else did, and on the day in question, Rove had a beer in front of him. The Cubs were on TV. The author tried to act casual. He spent ages looking at Wrigley Field, hoping the ivy might tell him what to do. He wanted to throw a drink in Rove's face. To ask a lot of questions about psychographics and WMDs and who really came up with the phrase "enhanced interrogation" anyway, and was it Yoo? Rumsfeld? That asshole Frank Luntz? There was an involved fantasy about finding the exact right combination of words, and all of a sudden Rove would be crying and overcome with regret and ready to have a heart attack right there in the middle of the bar while everyone pointed but nobody did anything, maybe because they were stricken or maybe because they knew who he was. Underlying the fantasy was also, of course, a feeling of guilt regarding his (meaning the author's) own arrogance, the sense that he thought he was even possibly important enough to have any kind of an impact on anything and also a fear that, deep down, maybe he wanted Rove to like him.

The author did want Bush to like him. That was a fact. Ever since he'd watched him throw out the first pitch of Game 3 of the World Series at Yankee Stadium while wearing a bulletproof vest that had to weigh like 15 pounds, and imagine trying to get your shoulder in the air, and the pitch was a perfect goddamn strike, and this was after 9/11, and holy shit you should've seen it. Maybe he should talk about that with Rove, the author thought, but then he didn't. Rove was getting up by that point. The author made a sudden movement. Rove motioned to the bartender and then to the author's drink (a Bell's Two Hearted Ale), and he sort of smirked and half-nodded, and the author didn't say no. He thinks about that a lot. That he didn't say no. He let Karl Rove buy him a beer and even finger-waved a thank you, and how complicit this makes him in the entire 21st century is something he's still trying to process.

MODEL UN

There's a story about a University of Minnesota student who hacked into the United Nations website. She was a sophomore from Mendota Heights. I think I had a class with her. A lot of people make that claim, I suppose, but maybe in my case it's true, and I don't really know. What she did was remove the digital meeting record of a UN Security Council session pertaining to nuclear non-proliferation and replace it with a transcript taken from a Model UN conference held in Columbus, OH. The scenario was generally the same. The conference was a large one, and students from all across the country attended. The University of Iowa was there. Oberlin. Yale. There were tensions between the US and Russia (this is in the model session now), and the NATO countries talked a big game, but they were mostly concerned with preserving the status quo, and, of course, Iran came up, and so did North Korea, and at one point everyone was fighting about Israel. Maybe that's why nobody noticed the switch. Poor kid, really, she goes to all this trouble and thinks she's making some kind of big political point, and then it's just business as usual. Like nothing ever happened, and she probably should've just quit right there. We all agree on that. She should've just packed it all in and kept the story as like a personal souvenir, a badge of honor kind of thing, but instead, she switched the document again, and this time she jazzed it up a little. The US Ambassador implied that Putin had slept with her husband. A member of the Chinese delegation was caught on a hot mic claiming that France had "welched" on a promise, and a member of the UK team, who was apparently Welsh himself, took offense. The Chinese member then tried to blame the translator. Things got ugly. The entire session devolved into a 15-door farce centered on lies and deceit and dirty little secrets (and also the nature of language, rhetoric, and especially the word "affair"), and that'll get 'em going, thought the hacker, but still. Nothing. Which meant she didn't really have a choice. She went nuclear. Uploaded one more document, and this one was a non-proliferation agreement. She used the Adobe suite to forge a few signatures. The United States agreed to decrease its atomic stockpile by 90% in exchange for a Russian promise to do the same (only by 91%), and the Chinese consented to taking a more aggressive stance toward North Korea, and somehow the Council also ended up unanimously approving a resolution returning Israel to pre-1967 borders and establishing a permanent Palestinian homeland, and who knows exactly which part of that finally did it, but the story blew up. It didn't take long to figure out it was a fake. Some sort of collegiate prank, and I guess the student fled to Namibia. Every so often there's a note in the alumni magazine about someone who got a postcard from Windhoek, and they always swear it's from her (people are constantly floating the idea of collecting all these postcards (assuming they can be found) and then putting up some kind of collage at the Weisman, and even if they're all frauds, the argument goes, it would be a hell of a commentary on myth and legend and artifactual fiction), and it's pretty cheeky the way we all talk about it now, but the Pentagon didn't like it. Neither did anyone else. Nobody official anyway, and the House and the Senate and the Oval Office all lit up with speeches about respect. Terror. Tragedy. The networks got somber, and the national security apparatus used words like "deranged," "disgraceful," and "derelict," and, "Whatever else it is," they assured us, "this whole story isn't the least bit funny."

RED STATES

My brother was 20 years older. Whole different generation. He had a heart attack at 58, and the whole town came to the funeral. 400 people. Me and Erin stood in the middle of this empty, nowhere gym and shook hands for hours. Unfamiliar hands. Hands we'd never met. All of them were hard and attached to long sleeves and red hats and red eyes, and we kept searching the faces for defiance or maybe scorn, but all we got was something stoic. A story. They told us how Jim did stitches at 3 a.m. and wrote all the right scripts, and sometimes he'd serve as this kind of emergency veterinarian for cows and horses and pigs, and yeah, we said. We nodded. That sounded like him alright, and they gave us lemon cakes and casseroles and sent us back to the city with a whole bunch of old-fashioned country compassion, and some of those casseroles are still in the freezer. I open it up sometimes. Pre-dawn or post-midnight. They got ice crystals and this weird sort of tuna fish smell, and I wouldn't eat that shit in a million years, but I like how Erin puts it. Her voice gets all cloudy through the phone, and she says everybody's gotta be reminded where they come from. Even if there's no way in hell they're ever going back.

D.

ASKING PRICE

Heard this from a colleague, back when I first got my real estate license, and he said, listen. After enough open houses, there's one thing I know, and that's there's always gonna be a guy in the basement. The unfinished part. Checking the walls for grout or signs of water damage, and the book on this guy is you just ignore him. He doesn't want the place. What he wants is to catch you in a lie, to start people thinking about guts and shit and poisoning the whole idea, the whole impression of the goddamn sale, and so you give him something real polite if you have to, something about how professional the job looks or how it's got the sump to end all sumps, but otherwise it's nothing. Cold shoulder. Do not give him any kind of room to operate, and I learned this the hard way once, over in Bettendorf, and this is in a real seller's market. Peak seller. Houses moving like mad and for 20% over list, and I've got this place all queued up. 270 appraisal and 295 ask, and there's people parked all the way around the block. Neighborhood's fucking packed. Droves. Hornets. Goddamn feeding frenzy or whatever, and most of 'em are fawning over countertops or whatever the hot thing was back then, and I'm thinking maybe it was the railyard backsplash or that time skylights were all the rage, and I hear voices downstairs. I'm sure you know this. How voices give away everything. You can tell who wants what and how bad and find every skeptical husband or aunt or father-in-law six miles off, and I go down there, and it's two guys. Look practically homeless. One of them is asking the other how much he got paid to be there, and the other one says, "A hair over 150," and they both laugh, and it turns out there's four people on the staircase hearing this conversation same as me, only they don't know it's a joke. Can't tell it's bullshit. They're whispering and sleeve-tugging, and the two basement guys start talking about how, look, we're in the middle of a goddamn drought, and these walls still feel damp, and the place goes empty like that. So fast you can't even notice. Socks sliding on real dark oak and these old-fashioned Midwestern types actually forgetting to hold the door on the way out, and it's a ghost town. A real fucking stampede, and I ask these guys, I say, "Hey, man, what the fuck," and "we're trying to make a living here," but all they do is just laugh some more. They sound like oilmen. Like miners or land speculators, and "Free country," says one of them, while the other's all eyes on me. Practically winks. He's going bald, going gray, and "Yeah," he says, leaning against the wall. "It's free to fuck up however you like."

IMITATION CHEDDAR

I made friends with an old guy once. At the community college. We were both in this speech class that started at 7:50 a.m., and we'd smoke outside until the very last second, and I was 21, he must have been 45. Worked the deli at Kowalski's. Sometimes, he'd bring leftover cheese, and maybe the best speech I ever heard was him talking about Gouda. Went on for 15 minutes. Was supposed to be a four-minute impromptu. But there he is up there rambling on about the aging process and passing out samples of one-year and seven-year and twelve-year while the professor looks pissed and impatient and too afraid or maybe too polite to cut him off, and then he gets into this whole riff about how the customers, they always wanna feel real fucking fancy, and so sometimes what he does is put the brand name label on some cheap generic trash, and nobody ever notices. All they do is go ahead and pay 18.99 a pound for some $4 Crystal Farms shit he's sliced up to look real nice, and he pictures them taking it home and talking about bite and wine pairings and rolling it around on their tongues as if they have any fucking clue, and the best part is he just pockets the difference. Store's no wiser, and the customers aren't after the cheese anyway, and what they really want is just to spend the money and feel that "Big Midwest Dream" sitting there in the cheap plastic, and everybody wins, he says. Keeps him in cigarettes, and we all got our own little hustles, don't we,

71

and about three weeks later he stops showing up for class. No message or nothing. Just disappears, and that wasn't unusual, of course, not at a place like that, and people got burned out or couldn't hack it, or maybe they had a kid or died or went back to jail, and I did go to Kowalski's, though. Trying to track him down. I hit every one within 15 miles, and I walk straight up to the counter and ask for Mike, for Mickey, for the guy with long brown hair and lines on his face, and the customers stare, and a couple of the managers, they tell me to fuck off.

"If you're looking to score, you're in the wrong place, pal," says one guy, and I act like I'm gonna hock a loogy, but I don't. I keep it in. We lock eyes for like one of them split seconds or whatever, and I call him an asshole. "Fuck," I say. As if I could ever forget.

EXPORT BUSINESS

There's this local legend about the Duluth Ship Canal, and it involves a group of residents coming down to the harbor with shovels and picks and all on their own. 1871. Superior, which sits right across the bay, doesn't like this. They want control over the port. Without a canal, the most natural outlet is on their side of the lake, and there are economics in play here. Ships. Cargo. Freight. So, they go off to court and file an injunction, except, the problem is, they're already too late. Canal's finished. The people of Duluth have been digging all night and every night. Been digging constantly for months. Headlamps. Blisters. They've been working in shifts and sleeping and playing cards in these tents pitched in the mud, and maybe it's entrepreneurial or maybe it's devious, and Horace Van Allen is one of these men. Nineteen years old. He'll go on to have a daughter who'll have a son who will himself have a daughter who'll give birth to a girl named Rion, and, at 12, she'll read about the ship canal on a field trip to the Lake Superior Marine Museum and then go home and ask her mother and get all these stories about duty and civics and togetherness. About how none of those men ever had to buy a drink in this town ever again, and they damn near couldn't set foot in Superior (and they say an army of drunk old Badgers would use decommissioned cannons to launch crumpled up overalls filled with piss and nails if they even got as far as

Park Point) without being torched and hunted and chased by desperate mobs, but that's not how Horace remembered it. He remembered the cold. Ground barely thawed. Leaning on a wooden handle and thinking about how the Natives were at rest in pre-Columbian mounds and scattered across Dakota Territory, and it was the Settlers who were restless. Impatient and on edge and maybe he didn't actually think this. Maybe it was something that occurred to him later (say, in 1890, when they sent him underground with nothing but a pickax and a crew claiming to have a shitload of Ojibwe blood) and he only imagined imagining it at the time, and the awareness of History, of Philosophy, the picturing of his own, individual agency as part of some collective momentum, a lurching forward, as part of what some would call Progress, that was all abstract and detached, but he was more confident in the tactile. The memories he could touch. Someone from one of the shipping companies slipping some scrip into his hand. Hardtack that seemed like it was left over from the Civil War. Two buddies on his shovel crew who got pneumonia and nearly died, and he could feel their breathing, their coughs, flecks of something invisible landing on his shoes while they told jokes about the intelligence of Swedish girls and passed around bourbon and coffee at 2 a.m., and sometimes the owners of small mining or lumber operations would give speeches and then try to sing these old railroad songs or sea chanties, and none of them could seem to find a shovel themselves (let alone the goddamn key), and he'd curl up in his tent and have nightmares about it. Silent ones. Even years later. There'd be waves crashing into his knees and water filling the line he was working on, and then it would all rise up to his neck while Jay Cooke watched and laughed, and Horace would wake up just dying of thirst, but he never did get those free drinks. They sent him out to the ore mines after that. Gave him a job, and he lived in the dark. Dug iron. Lost his hearing and then died of something that was probably lung cancer in 1912, but he was already a hero by then. In all of the stories they tell.

PEOPLE, AT HEART

The neighbors had this daughter who turned 13 and started to think she was Anne Frank reincarnate, and she'd learned Dutch, they said. German too. They found some red-checkered diary in a dresser drawer and didn't dare open it, and at first, they thought about sending her out to Fargo for some kind of psychiatric evaluation, but then one night they get drunk and listen to crickets and the way the corn hisses and pops in the field after traffic dies down on the old highway, and the wife says they should lean in. Let it pass. Avoid creating one of them parent-child dynamics where requests are mocked and orders automatically negated, and the husband builds this room on the upper floor of their barn. It takes him ages on account of there's almost no fiber out here, and the connection is always horrible, and none of them have a passport, let alone the time (or the money (or even the desire)) to travel to Amsterdam, and so he pores over webpages. Google Earth. It's one pixel at a time, and he takes virtual tours and is real painstaking about it because he needs it to look right, to feel real, and eventually he figures out how to arrange the furniture like just so. Exactly the same. And, as he does it, he thinks he notices these particular structural and perhaps dimensional similarities between his barn and that annex above Opekta, the place where old what's-her-name helped hide the family, and it's something in the way the sun hits. The Feng Shui.

The casting of shadows and the arc the dust traces as it falls from the shelves to the floor, and the daughter doesn't notice this, but she does spend time up there. Sometimes brings friends. She reads essays, mostly, and also poems, and she draws pictures of these castles that look half-finished, or maybe like they're infested with crows (and for a while she's posting photos and sharing clips, and there's a moment when it all threatens to go viral, but then (like mostly everything else) it doesn't), and, one day, she stops going. Cold turkey and here today, gone tomorrow, and, of course, this was the plan all along, but the husband, he can't help but feel a little pissed off, a little confused, and he doesn't want to ask her about it, and so he starts taking these night walks up there by himself. Spends whole evenings. Shuffling and reshuffling cards and somehow never winning at solitaire, and his side of the bed grows cold, and the wife is wondering how in the fuck it's always left to her to keep everything together ("and isn't that just the way of the world"), and she finally snaps him out of it by refinancing the whole goddamn property to buy a couple of vintage Ford Mustangs (or maybe it was some sort of decommissioned military aircraft, an F-86 Sabre or something) he can fix up in his spare time, and the room sits empty. People talk about it. Kids at school. Younger brothers and sisters and uncles and cousins of the daughter's original set of friends, and some of these people sneak up there. Throw some books around. Move the bed. They leave behind beer cans and used-up joints, condoms and gum wrappers and copies of Men's Health or Sports Illustrated, and this rumor starts that the place is a meth lab. A crack den. It's some kind of sanctuary for illicit sex and illegal immigrants, or else it's one of them cartel distribution hubs, and most of this stuff gets spread in basements and parking lots and all offline and through unofficial channels, but that doesn't mean they aren't monitored, these channels, and there are Authorities out there in the æther. Big ones. Waiting and listening, and there are nights when the air's all static and humid and tinged, and one stray word of Spanish could set the whole barn alight.

SCARECROW JO

Back before he quit, Morgan had to take these trips out to chicken farms all along I-80 and do a bunch of inspections. Head counts and the like. He hated it, and the farmers hated him, and he always rushed back east doing 90 the whole way, except whenever he was really out there, as in like way out toward the Panhandle, he'd go ahead and book a room somewhere right around North Platte on account of this bartender there. Waitress maybe. Real skinny, he said. Black hair and blue eyes, and that was all you could ever get him to say, and she once bet him a week's worth of tips you could hear corn growing. As in like literally hear it, and she takes him out to this field after last call, and they've been bombing Windsor all night, and by some fucking miracle she can hold it a whole lot better than him, and he's stumbling. Tripping over stalks barely come up to your shins, and this is how you know he's telling the truth is nothing happens. They sit out there. They wait. It's cloudy, he says, and humid, and he starts trying to tell her about his divorce, about how like you should never trust a woman who wants a real diamond ring, and she keeps putting up a finger. Telling him to shut it. They hear these pops intermittently. Static. It sounds like the AM band between Kearney and Cozad, and she says, "If you come out here a week after planting time and kneel with your hands at your sides, them stalks will be brushing your fingertips before you can spit, and that's what you city folk are never gonna understand is it really does move fast out here." It's gotta. On account of progress and money and appetites, and Morgan, he does get on his knees. He closes his eyes. He reaches for her hand, only she's already gone and so is his wallet, and he sleeps out there, he says. Waiting and listening, and somewhere in the noise is headlights. A code. It's a little prairie prophecy, and we all laugh about how he says he'll call us just as soon as he does the calculations, and we picture him writing. Typing. Sitting on his ass and going wild with meaning, and what we're really thinking is how all them sounds are a load of bullshit, and get with it, man. There's only so much they're ever gonna let you hear.

NIGHT HOUSE

His senior year, Danny finally gets a room with a private shitter, and there's Eugene McCarthy sitting on it, certain nights, 2:15 a.m. Maybe it's McCarthy's ghost. Danny wouldn't know the difference. Honestly, he doesn't recognize who McCarthy is (and if he heard the name, he'd probably think Jenny and not even Joe), and his first thought is some old monk's gone senile. Started wandering the campus at night. He wants to call security, but he's also got a few stray ounces of weed hanging out in a drawer, and you never know what might happen when you invite those fuckers into your room, and so he and McCarthy light up. Run the shower fan to dissipate the smoke. McCarthy says, "I should've got myself clubbed in '68, you know. Should've stuck it right up Humphrey's ass."

"I got hit with a bat once," says Danny. "Well, part of one. Fluke thing. It was this minor league baseball game, and some tomahawk splinter comes flying into the stands, and my mom thought I was dead. Just laid there bleeding from my forehead, and when I woke up everything smelled like hot dogs, I think. Brewed tea. Or that's how she tells it anyway."

"Dying can make you a hero, kid. Take it from a guy who knows," and they go on like this for a while. McCarthy, who Danny starts calling Pops, he's got something detached about him, something not quite ready to air, and Danny falls asleep on the floor. When he wakes up, McCarthy's gone. Doesn't come back for three nights, and then it's five, and then he shows up two nights in a row. The seventh time they see each other is a blizzard. The buses have stopped running to the women's campus 5 miles down the road, and the two of them can hear footsteps tearing up the stairs. Shouting. Everything echoes off the cinderblock, and eventually security does show up. Two of them. They find Danny cross-legged in the bathroom while McCarthy sits on the throne, and, "What the fuck is this?" one of the officers says.

"Looks like a goddamn séance."

"Gene here's my uncle," says Danny, even though it's clear no one believes him. "Ain't that right, Pops?"

"What in the hell is wrong with him?"

"Can't he shit by himself?"

"He's not shitting," says Danny. "It's like sciatica or something. Bad back. Needs to have the right angle. Center of gravity sort of thing."

"Jesus, the guy looks fucking dead."

"People think I'm dead," says Gene. "A lot of them. Been buried so many times, I just about lost count," and with that, there he goes. Gone again. Security stands there looking at each other. They don't have a fucking clue, but word gets passed up the chain pretty quick, and then there's administration camped out in Danny's room. The president. Provost. Two guys from advancement, and they understand it's McCarthy almost immediately. Maybe they know before they even get there. Having parsed the accounts and arranged the pieces and always understood alumni. Selling them. Promoting them. Encapsulating everything the prospective family needs to know.

"We should sell tickets," says the president, though the others worry it's not exactly on brand. There are references to ambience. Stench. Thoughts about dignity and decorum and the personality makeup of the applicant pool, though the president keeps invoking "undervalued markets." "Ways around the demographic cliff." Gene shows up one night to hear them talk about all this, long after Danny's been (forcibly?) relocated, and he hopes they do invite people in. Make a little museum out of it. Folks all lined up and desperate to live history, and he'll tell them what's what. Make sure they get their money's worth. Or maybe what he'll do is figure out a way to make the pipes overflow, to hover above burst lines and sewage backup, the whole of the American diet and its sprawling microbiome, and it'll be seeping through the subfloor. Dripping these little rancid puddles on everyone down below, and he pictures this. Wonders about protest. About meaning. Administrative vocal chords are vibrating all around him and at frequencies fairly fucked-up, and the word they keep coming back to is product. Value. Exchange, and Gene keeps his mouth shut because he can't form the message exactly, but what he really wants to tell them involves waste. Certain forms of it, and let's call it institutional plumbing. Let's just say it's the price of admissions control.

WIND IN THE WIRES

In Duluth, the boys will take you to Lake Superior at sunset and tell you about the Edmund Fitzgerald. This is a known thing. They have these music rehearsal rooms in the basement of the Performing Arts Center at UMD, and sometimes instead of trumpets and pianos and saxophones, you can hear voices. Practicing. Ups and downs and the precise way to talk about death so that it inspires reverence and awe and desire. Hunger. These guys all figure there's some kind of combination of soundwaves that's bound to be an aphrodisiac, to create whatever level of danger and/or attraction will let them feel you up on the rocks near the harbor, and they trade tips and details with each other in the dining halls and bars and locker rooms after practice, and there are all these various references to Gordon Lightfoot, or taconite, or how they once bribed an altar boy (and sometimes it's even a priest) up at St. Peter's to ring the bells 29 times at precisely 7:10 p.m. on November the 10th, and nobody knows if any of this is true. If it's all bluster. Some kind of St. Louis County legend run amok, and girls roll their eyes when they hear about it. I'm telling you, they do. They think how there's no way that could work, and seduction by ghost story (by fucking oral tradition) sounds about as quaint as maritime lore, as sea shanties and ship canals, and they don't even mine taconite anymore (though some of the really granola ones will make snide remarks about how we're all still drinking the runoff, and they'll also probably mention cancer clusters and North Country and how what passed for feminism back in 2005 was letting Charlize Theron get harassed for chasing mesothelioma all the way across the Iron Range), and they're pretty sure they can tell when some asshole's putting them on, and, the truth is, they can. That's undeniable. And, of course you'll recognize it, goes the response, on account of it'll be beyond fucking obvious and typically male transparent, but that's not the point. The point is, the story's good. It gets under your skin. It's something about the way the water looks when it's all black and still and frigid and how the whole town smells like damp barley, and these boys are the same as the tourists in Canal Park (who you'll also learn to recognize in a flash and without really thinking) in that they maybe see it but can only express it cheaply, in practiced soliloquies or parkas from Duluth Trading, and you won't sleep with them. You won't even be tempted. But you will remember the story. Picture a boat taking on water. Canada and First Nations and fur traders, and you'll look up at the moon and swear your own death is somewhere in the legend, in the buildings, in how this combination of light and cold and moisture makes the place feel like it's both 1871 and 2269, and it's some kind of prophecy, and you won't be able to leave until you understand. Until it's done with you, and the boys are just a gateway. A highway. An on-ramp to America and all the little shards that might somewhere still be left.

SPAM FACTORY

We ate cans of the stuff during the '85-'86 strike. Dad smuggled them out of the plant starting maybe six months prior. One at a time. He sensed it all coming, and so it was every smoke break and every lunch, and his whole life he never took vacation or sick leave or nothing, and we had a room in the basement. It looked like a bomb shelter. Sometimes, my brother Jeff and I would play Monopoly or Risk down there, and when we started, the shelves were all packed, and we thought we'd maybe get through a game or two, but then it was weeks later. Nearly a year. Dad began keeping inventory, and Mom canceled the cable, and when the bank took the house, we only had the one can left. Mom died, and Dad tried to give it to Jeff. "I don't want that shit," he said, but that was later. On the phone. To me.

I let him drive it over one night, Marie and the kids at her sister's over in Rochester, and we drank a few Grain Belts, and I got that can in the hall closet. Where we keep the jackets. Winter comes, and you see it every day, and sometimes I'll tell Jeff how it's a wonder he ever won at Monopoly on account of you gotta understand collection and culture and how there's this value in like ironic or maybe nostalgic consumption, and I'll get the call one day. I know I will. Might be the governor of Hawaii, or maybe the curator at that new museum downtown, and they're all gonna want it of course, and I've got the price all set in terms of backpay and punitive damages, and I guess I'll probably give it to them if they meet it, but here's the difference between me and Jeff. He don't really remember. I can say exactly what it cost.

L.

PAUL BUNYAN DELUXE

In Brainerd, you can hire a haruspex for bachelor parties. It's part of a package. Comes with a cabin and a keg and sometimes live (and recorded) entertainment, and what the guy does is serve as a hunting guide, and the first deer or duck or rabbit or whatever, he'll read its guts. None of this is advertised. You have to know who to ask. What he does is cut the thing open and toss the liver, and it's gotta travel at least 15 feet on account of some ancient Viking tradition, and then he studies it for a while. Looks for sacred marks. He makes some predictions about marriage, the Best Man, or if the Bears will cover the spread, and often these predictions are dark. Somehow violent. Everyone just nods soberly while he recites them, and he wears a wolf pelt that's mostly for show. He leaves when he's done. The party can do what it likes with the animal. Then, they all adjourn to the lake. They drink and fire up the big screen or maybe even bring in some real live women. In the morning, somebody wakes up and dry heaves into the bathroom sink. It sounds like a farm animal. A chicken or a goose or something else avian. You can hear it all through the cabin. It doesn't wake anybody up exactly, but everyone's aware of it on some level. Synapses fire. Myelin lights up. There's some brief and unconscious electrochemical warfare over consequences and oracular hangovers, but that dies out pretty quick, and they all head home thinking it's all in good fun. They're thinking how none of it's really worth a second thought.

A BETTER MOUSETRAP

Sam and I, we had rodent issues, so we walked down to the hardware store and tried to sort them out.

"Glue traps," he said. "Only way to fly."

I told him they starve in those. Sometimes chew through their own legs. They scream, and I guess it bores its way into your skull. They say you never can forget the sound.

"Yeah, okay, Tee, you're probably right. Wouldn't want to hurt the bastards, now would we? Better to have 'em running across your face while you sleep." Sam, he could be a real asshole sometimes. Other times, though, he'd make dinner. It wasn't fancy, and there were always cans involved. Cans and ketchup. He'd still put on an apron and toss me beers from the fridge while I sat there feet up, and when I dropped one, he wouldn't even flinch.

I forget if that's what he did that night, or if he said sorry or what, but we put the traps in the corners and all around the kitchen. Lined a few up near the bed. We probably bought a couple extra packs, and they stayed that way for a week, but you could still hear feet scratching inside the walls. Especially at night. I said, "It's kind of nice, isn't it? Like once you get used to it?" He shook his head a few times, and when I came home from work the next day, the traps were gone.

"Giving up?" I said.

"Nah, we caught 'em all, Tee. Whole crew. Must've been at least five."

"Alright."

"I took 'em out to the trash like the package said. Put 'em all out their misery first, of course, have no fear," and he popped some gum as he said it, only it didn't sound right. Didn't sound like him, and, later, after we watched this movie about a woman who could deliver messages from the dead, he nodded off. Woke up screaming. I'd never seen that before, and so I got tense and mumbled how it was okay, baby, and then I stared at the wall. The scratching was still there, except quieter somehow, as if they were mourning. As if there was one less mouse they didn't know how to find.

CLEAN-UP CREW

Mrs. Horowitz has a barn full of animal skeletons. It's the small ones mostly. Mice and voles and fish. She'll pay you 125 for a new specimen, as long as it's clean and complete and in good condition. What she does is use them on her anatomy students. The gifted kids. Track 1A and AP, and it's all this real special kind of final exam. She throws the bones in a bucket, I think, or maybe it's a trough or a barrel or something, and she puts the kids in groups, and she'll tell 'em something like, "This tub here's a sunfish, a raccoon, and a cat got clipped by a Volkswagen in 1987," and they gotta put 'em all together no mistakes. First team to finish gets an A, and then it's all downhill from there, and me and ol' Evo couldn't hack it, not by a longshot, and so we keep our eyes out for fresh kills. The rare and newly dead. There's a few other groups around town always try to get in on the action, and it's mostly real friendly-like, but the other day we find this bald eagle, and Scottie from the Cub store is there at the same time, and we let it lay there between us, and it's all knives out and icy stares, and "I'll flip you for it," he says, and we nod. We wait. Evo's got this Eisenhower silver dollar he always insists on, but Scottie wants a quarter he found by the old railroad tracks back when he was 12. The procedure here is simple.

"We toss 'em both," says Evo, "And if they're the same it's us, but if they're different it's you," and Scottie's alright with that, and so up they go. Spinning. Twisting. Ours ends up heads, and his lands on the fucking bird, and we walk over there real quiet and real pained, and when it's tails, we watch him throw the thing into the cab of his truck.

"Gentle, asshole," I say, and he laughs. Drives off. It's only later we think about America, and then we're drinking coffee and Kahlua at this shitty folding table out on his deck.

"Better it's Scottie, really," says Evo, on account of something about symbols. Hexes. Something about stripping all that beauty just so some egghead can feel good about putting it back together. Hooking a cheap scholarship. Grabbing herself a taste of that delicious college debt.

FUR TRADE DAYS

We shot a beaver back behind the old Donaldson place and then didn't know what to do with it. Nobody had a license. Tenpin said he thought there were a few recipes from back in the day, and it was mostly stews and shit. Old-fashioned, North Country cuisine, but what we did in the end was call this guy John Boy Ray, and he knew how to skin 'em. Tan the pelts. We paid him 50 or so each to make a hat out of it. Gave it to Pedersen for his bachelor party, and you should've seen his face when he opened the box. We were fucking laughing about the last beaver you'll ever see, and he looked hungover and gassed up and thrilled all at once. He wrote us each a goddamn thank you note if you can believe it. They came in the mail three weeks later and weren't even in Vicki's handwriting, and last I heard she got it in the divorce. Didn't even fucking want it. Just put it on the list out of spite and on account of he supposedly slept with her sister, and I don't know what happened. I try to stay out of it. What I do is keep my ear to the ground, and someone said the other day she never uses it. Keeps it in some trunk all winter. It's the warmest thing in six counties, and there it sits just gathering dust, and then she brings it out when the sister comes over. Thanksgiving. Christmas. Hangs it on this hook in the front room and stares at everyone all vengeful and high on moral superiority, and we tell Pedersen not to worry. Dodged a bullet. We'll get you another one eventually, and that's exactly the problem with some women. They act like they never done nothing wrong themselves.

LAS VACAS

Every so often, one of the fieldhands will kill a few cows and carve strange marks into the flanks, and this happens irregularly. Without pattern. That doesn't stop folks from trying to find one, though (a pattern, I mean), and they'll say how it's always right around a marriage, or maybe a divorce, or else the second full moon after the first Sunday post-All-Star Break, and Benito eats baked beans straight from the can and tells me his grandfather's the one who did it first, and what all our fieldhands do then is set up camp on that hill out near the Stevens' place and keep watch. Tell stories. Stories about brushfires and coyotes and women, and they get real drunk and settle old scores with arm-wrestling matches, and the bosses let this go on because they believe in release. Tradition. Might even be that they're the ones who start to whisper to each other when the discontent picks up, when there's lawsuits in the air, or maybe talk of unions, of walkoffs, of hiding these leaky cans of Roundup beneath certain, highly placed mattresses, and "Call the ICE line," one of them will say, and the game is that the others have to react. Calm him down. Smoke a few cigars. Maybe they play cards in that barn that ain't got no roof, and "Nah," one of them says. "All we really need is to call in the Vacas," and that's the phrase they send on down the chain, and the next thing you know a couple of cows are gone. Mangled. Thousands of dollars flushed. The bosses pretend to be all panicked while the search party gets rung, and it's everyone and his brother searching. His uncle. Out there bonding and laughing and distracted, and the bosses, well, they make a big show of putting all the women and children in basements, and we share our own stories about vampires and la "chupavaca," and Benito is real public about how it's all the work of them extraterrestrials, but then he leans over, hand on my knee. He says, "What the bosses don't know is we got the real thing in a cage, and we're gonna let her out when the timing's right. When every last one of them thinks it's all to his advantage, then one night it won't be cattle you find in the pasture."

"Promise?" I say, and he does. We shake hands. Swear secrets. You can hear a door slamming in the wind, and I imagine Tanner's old man in the moonlight. Reaching for his shotgun. There's green arms in front of him. Spikes. Scales and flesh and teeth, and he's scared shitless. His fat-ass fingers are twitching and way more than a second too late.

STATE OF NATURE

Best guess is two, maybe three years from now, a consortium of biologists, entomologists, and activists will use sophisticated environmental modeling software to infer the existence of a heretofore undiscovered species of insect whose habitat covers hundreds of thousands of square miles of Amazon rainforest. This insect will be nocturnal. Reclusive. Unseen and only identifiable thanks to extensive analyses of soil composition, fungal activity, and (various types of) night monkey stool samples that will show small but statistically significant deviations from expectations as calculated by ALDO, an advanced algorithm designed to "digitally map the vast chunks of the biosphere that are, as of yet, untouched by human development (and often even unseen by the human eye)." These deviations will be explainable only through the presence of said insect (and, okay, perhaps also and additionally others within the same genus), and, working backward (and using everything they know about decomposition rates, erosion, the metabolic processes and basic microbiome and digestive anatomy of night monkeys, etc.), the aforementioned consortium will be able to use ALDO to reverse-engineer a kind of schematic for this particular insect. ALDO will even draw a full-color photograph, and this insect will look rather ordinary. Perhaps a bit uglier. It will lack the grace of, say, a praying mantis, or the raw menace of a Japanese giant hornet, and instead resemble an uncommonly large cricket, not dissimilar (its size excluded) from what any toddler might find in a typical North American yard. This will, of course, be a problem for the consortium, given that their working theory is that this insect is (in addition to being existentially threatened by Amazonian deforestation) critical to the entire ecosystem, a staple part of the diet of any number of primate (and an ancillary part of the diet of any number of rodent) species, whose stool (thanks, primarily, to said insect) ultimately plays an integral role in sustaining soil composition (and, therefore, in the existence of any number of species of tree, which, of course and in turn, play a vital role in the reduction of global CO_2 emissions and the maintenance of a healthy troposphere). As such, it must be protected from incursions by logging companies and other commercial and industrial outfits, and legal cases tend to be won (and injunctions granted) on the basis of, let's say, the aesthetic qualities of a particular species, like polar bears. Spotted owls. Exotic game animals. Still, the insect (which some will refer to as the Salinger and others, perhaps more radical in orientation, will call the Pynchon) will be the best hope for any kind of "Save the Rainforest" victory, and so the consortium will have to acknowledge that any picture drawn by ALDO will, obviously, be speculative, and therefore contain sources of uncertainty, and so they will carefully use probabilistic methods to assign a 95-percent CI to factors like "cuteness" and "gut-level fear induction" and, simply, "edge," and manip-ulate the image in such a way as to ensure that it both fits within the stated range and inspires attachment. Emotional response. Protective instincts, etc., and focus groups will be convened for this specific purpose. Psychological profiles of circuit (including appeals and even Supreme as well as various international) court judges will be completed. So, also, will in-depth analyses (some of which will be done by ALDO) of law review articles and amici, and all in an effort to produce the image most likely to lead to legal victory, temporary or (hopefully) otherwise. Once created, said image will be Exhibit A when reporters are notified that lawsuits have been filed all up and down the supply chain, in Manaus and Milwaukee and Manhattan, and there will be a series of arguments and a mélange of rulings, and injunctions will be imposed and then denied, lifted and reinstated, and the global cost of paper (as well as lumber and a host of other lumber-dependent products) will double not so much because of any real interruption to production and distribution as because of the perception (the "opportunity," as some will argue) of one, and nobody on the ground will know whether or not cutting (meaning, according to the consortium, "deforestation" (or, according to the more "radical" and/or "aggressive" organizations, "slash-and-burn destruction")) can happen on any given day, and it will be years (if not decades (indeed, if not eternity)) before any kind of final and globally uniform ruling is issued and any sort of agreement reached, during which time there will be articles and arguments about value and "conservation" (and if a tree falls in the forest or an insect invisibly exists, and, you know, what's really the difference between this CGI cricket or whatever and, say, something done by DreamWorks or Pixar or any other cutting-edge animation studio) and also massive increases in anxiety surrounding just about every issue you can imagine (related and (seemingly) not), and, no, this bug won't technically know exactly what is going on, but we'll all have to surrender ourselves to the following fact: It understands the implications. More completely than every single one of us.

YEAR OF THE LIZARD

Dead of Minnesota winter, and my sister finds an iguana in a snowbank. Thing's frozen solid. We put it in a pillowcase, and the tail sticks out the top, and then we bike all the way out to Moorhead and keep hitting these ice chunks. The iguana goes flying. We have to find it all over again.

When we get to campus, we find the biology department. Some woman's there. She looks younger than you'd think, and she takes the thing into this back office, and I imagine she's got a microscope. A scalpel. My sister's sitting on a bench in the hallway, leaning against a glass case, and there's plants in there or something. Fungus. It all looks fake or calcified or I don't know what, and when the woman comes back out she says it's real.

"What do you mean?" I say. ,

"The iguana," she says, and it's clinical. All fucking business. We look at her like she's got four heads because of course it's real, and we can tell dead from plastic, and then she tells us it was a girl. "Female," she says. Just laid eggs. I don't know how she knows that. Don't ask either. It's only later when I think that maybe she's fucking with us, and maybe she isn't even a biologist, or at least not a very good one anyway, but my sister, she's never been happier. Spends the whole ride back smiling off into space, and we leave the iguana there, and I get phone calls. Years later. Mom and Dad die, and we sell the farm, and she puts a rider on the purchase agreement that says anybody finds an iguana any-where on the property it's got to be reported to this email she sets up just solely for that specific purpose, and the buyers, they find this whole thing charming if you can believe it. They let her onto the property whenever she's in town, two or three times a year, and I've only been with her the once, but there she is, digging in the dirt. Got binoculars. Looks real serious. Brings a camera and documents every search, year by year and visit by visit, and she says how iguanas are adaptable and invasive and communicative, and I try to tell her about pet stores and practical jokes, but she sticks with it firmly. Thorough. On her knees and combing the ground and telling anyone who'll listen oh, they're there alright. All you have to do is keep your eyes on the road.

IN THE OFFING

Van Allen works for the Minnesota Highway Patrol, and when he's on the late shift, he'll find dead animals everywhere. Racoons and shit. The stuff people hit and maybe don't even realize, or else they're drunk and worried it's a person, and so they just keep on going. Forget what happened. Maybe it'll disappear. What he does is call this buddy of his from Crosby, and the guy's tall and wears glasses and has some weird fucking obsession with hieromancy, and they'll look at these rodents and birds mostly and try to find the sacred organs. The lungs, the heart, the liver especially. The buddy hires himself out sometimes, but that's mainly just for show, and he always relishes these late-night calls from Van Allen. Can't fucking wait to hit the pavement at 3 a.m. and considers it his true vocation, and he never makes prophecies per se. It's more like checking for harmony. Bringing human attitude into congruence with divine whim, and it's all a matter of accretion, they decide. Patterns. Large enough samples. One night, they figure they'll be out on 371, and some hawk or skunk will throw everything into focus, and they'll sit there and have a cigar, and "You reckon what I reckon?" Van Allen will say, and the buddy will take his glasses off. He'll pinch his nose.

"Sure does seem like anger to me," he'll say, and Van Allen will wonder if they really needed all this data, all this death, just to get there, and maybe he'll even put it out there real direct, as in like, "Hey, Jesus, Dell, just what the fuck was this whole thing about anyway?" and Dell will shrug. He won't know any more than anyone else, but he'll spit on the ground and stuff some feathers into his pocket and tell whoever's listening that maybe there is no point, and that's the issue with oracles, isn't it.

"Sometimes you show up, and you're already twelve years too late."

O.

EL BÉTICO AUTÉNTICO

My brother got obsessed with soccer and bought a bunch of shit, shit that was mostly like t-shirts and subscriptions to whatever digital platforms let a person watch Boca Juniors and the Turkish Süper Lig and random Italians running around the field with their nipples hanging out, and Real Betis became his favorite. He adopted them. Probably because everyone else was in love with Barça or one of the Madrids, or else, more likely, someone from England, someone with a lot of Americans, and my brother taught himself Spanish. He read Andalusian poetry on the weekends. He spoke to us in Spanish. To himself. To his boss. He quit his job and bought a ticket to Sevilla, and we just knew it was gonna be one of those visa overstay type situations, and so we tried to make the most of the intervening months. We tried to get on his wavelength. We watched and ate tapas or whatever, and I remember going to Menard's with him. This was like a week before he left. I wanted a new dryer, and he ran up and down the aisles muttering, speaking, always loud but never quite yelling, "Viva el Betis," he said, "Manque pierda," and people were like what the fuck, man, you could tell, but this one guy. This one guy. Stopped my brother. Shook his hand. Whatever they said was drowned out by someone making I bet like a third set of keys, but it was probably in Spanish anyway, and this guy's eyes, they looked like they were sure. Like they knew. My brother,

I don't know, his heart must have been beating fast , and he looked back at me, and I looked over at the lumber. I thought about deck replacement and new flooring and how wood tells you everything, doesn't it? Its chips and divots and patterns. The way it casts shadows. I let those guys stand in them. I heard my brother cough. His new buddy cleared his throat, and yeah. Okay. I guess there was some fucking flash of idiot beauty in the two of them, standing there, each knowing exactly what the other wanted to pretend.

FAIR TRADE VALUE

In the basement of his parents' house, a man finds a baseball card. Unboxed. Stuck underneath an empty shelving
unit and covered in cobwebs, and it's Hector Comala, 2B,
Cincinnati Reds. Finished third in ROY voting back in '18,
and then went 4-for-37 the next April with 16 Ks and 12
scalded ground balls right into the teeth of the shift, and
he decides fuck it. I'm gonna bunt. The next 30 ABs. 50.
Whatever it takes. I'm gonna bunt and slap oppo squirmers
until they can't imagine playing anything but the traditional
defensive alignment, and he gets to do this for maybe five
games. Coaches are yelling at him the whole time. Front
office types. They got print outs and stat sheets, and the
logic is clear, see, and they tell him they believe in him. He'll
snap out of it. Hit the ball in the air, they say, and that's the
best way to beat the shift, and he knows this. Deep down,
he really does. It's just, the thing of it is, he hates the fucking shift that bad, hates its arrogance, its air of intellectual
superiority, and it reminds him of this statue back home in
Monterrey, and there's something about the way it looks
at you like it knows just exactly what you're thinking and
how it'll be covered in bird shit long after you're dead and
gone, and so, he keeps on bunting. Weak contact. Aiming
for these rollers just off the third-base line, and he manages
to scrape together a few hits and thinks he's starting to get
pretty good at it when suddenly, he takes a fastball off the

hand. 98 miles an hour. Broken hamate. Swears to this day it was fucking intentional and maybe set up by his own general manager, and after let's say about 8 weeks on the IL he's stashed down at Triple A and then never makes it back. The man, he doesn't remember any of this, looking at the card. He has no idea who Hector Comala even is. He stopped watching baseball decades ago, but, for some reason, he can't let go of the thing. Carries it around like a talisman. In his pocket, briefcase, under the pillow while he sleeps and whatever. He scours baseball history books and internet archives, and here's the funny thing, is this card? It's got Comala in the shift. 2B as not-exactly-shallow right field, and his cap's throwing shadow over his whole face, and the listed value on the thing is 76 cents, which doesn't seem right to the man holding it. He'd never sell, of course, but still. There are players who deserve more. Little futile revolutions that must be worth something, and not in this market, he thinks, though maybe there are anti-markets. Subterranean and waxing. Invisible forces. Currents like the one that lets a 1964 Curt Flood fetch somewhere around three grand, and the man, he talks to this card, at night. After the kids are asleep. He sets it up next to a Coors Light and says take heart, amigo, because the future is radical and process-oriented, and that's all fine enough for you, but my question is will I be around to see it. It's will I live to see the day, and sometimes, Comala, he talks back. The light bounces off the border and tells the man it's the wrong fucking question. For what you're talking about, he must be saying, it's got to be the imagining ends up its own sort of reward.

ALL DRESSED UP

For a while there my sister was gonna marry this guy named Aspen, and he always wore pink polos and smelled like one of them stores out at Crossroads. We took him deer hunting once. Stayed at this cabin up near Moorhead. Pop shot a doe on the second morning, and we all went to watch him dress it. Family tradition. Pop, he's a real pro, and there's almost like this beauty to the way he holds the knife. We always tell him how he should've been a butcher. How he makes it all seem sacred. Holy and magic and dignified.

Anyhow, we get out to the carcass, and Pop asks Aspen if he's ever done anything like this before, and all we hear is the poor bastard puking over behind some tree. Pop hasn't even made the first cut yet. Some of us want to laugh, you can tell, and maybe we do a little bit. Like just real quiet out the sides of our mouths, but, later, back at the cabin, I find Aspen back by the firepit. Everyone else is inside. Maybe napping, maybe tying one on. He's drinking a Grain Belt, and I don't touch him or nothing, but I do say not to worry. Like, hey, we all get that way, and the dirty little secret is nobody likes the gutting part, and my first kill Pop actually made me do it. Handed me the knife. Stood over my shoulder. I started crying when I had to cut the diaphragm, and he told me how we don't do this on account of it's fun. We do it because it's real. I told Aspen, I said, "I don't know what the fuck that means, but I still remember it. Think I might even believe it too."

He took a long pull. Screwed the bottle into the dirt. He didn't say nothing, but I could tell from his eyes he'd never really be my brother, and the only thing to do was promise not to hate him for it. To think about Cassie and how I might tell her it wasn't anything I could rightly explain, but I speak from experience, and I guess the thing of it is we are who we are. And there's certain jobs we just ain't man enough to do.

PLEXIGLASS MENAGERIE

One morning, out of nowhere, a big plexiglass case showed up on the quad. This was Saint John's University. Collegeville, Minnesota. Spring 2005. The thing was maybe 10x20. About 8 feet high. It had a door on the north side, and so the whole setup looked like a racquetball court. At times you'd even see people in there, playing racquetball. You'd glance out the window of your sociology classroom, and there'd be blue flying off the walls and two guys who ran track slamming into each other, and, at night, people would have sex. That was the rumor, anyway. That they'd sneak in, and freshmen would camp out in front of Mary Hall and shine lights on them, and most of the time the couples scattered, or else they'd pretend they were up to something else. It got to be like a strategy, and if you could manage to keep your clothes on, to keep the noise down, to find some shadowed corner and use the sides for leverage, then maybe you could get away with it. I guess somebody would clean it. Semi-regularly. At least, it often smelled like Windex, and a professor held a class in there once. Young guy. Freshly minted Ph.D. in economics, and it was supposed to be some kind of object lesson in overcrowding or resource allocation, and people gathered outside and peered in, and then one of them tied the door closed. The class started to panic. There was this girl who must have been a first-year, and she had braces and freckles and looked like she was probably from Lakeville, and she fainted, but there wasn't enough room to go horizontal, and so her face slumped and squished against the wall. You could see her cheek stretched flat. One of the football players said it looked like a pie crust or a rolled-out hunk of Play-Doh, and people thought they were losing oxygen. The professor sat lotus. He closed his eyes. Around him were screams and flip phones opening and closing and clattering on the floor, until finally somebody let them out. They carried the girl, but that wasn't exactly necessary, seeing as she'd only been unconscious for a few seconds. No harm done. A while later, this group of monks held a Mass in there, and there were a bunch of kids who liked to smoke weed and let the whole thing fill with haze. I never went inside. I wanted to, but so did everyone else, and there was never a moment—never an activity—that felt real and natural and like it needed to be performed. One night it was stacked wall-to-wall with beer cans and another night somebody barred the door, and every week there'd be more claims of ownership, people saying they created it, and there were all these theories about whether it was an art student or a philosophy major, and I guess they took it down because they figured somebody might die in there, that that would be the natural end point. There were people who swore someone already had. Their claims alternated between being credible and crazy. Nobody knows where the glass is now, but we always hit the quad during reunions, as we sit there drinking. We tell the same stories. We crawl and grab handfuls of dirt, and I swear to Christ there's still about a million spots where the grass is all yellow and trampled and flat.

EYE OF THE STORM

This is unverified. You should know that going in. There's some fragmentary evidence, of course: mostly archived webpages and bootleg videos and such, but the rest is basically hearsay and whole cloth invention, and it all involves this Grinnell grad from the 1990s, a guy by the name of Goins. He had an obsession with D3 basketball. Used to drive all across the Midwest with a handheld camera. One night he's up in the middle of nowhere, Minnesota, and St. John's beats St. Thomas at the buzzer, and half a dozen monks and a few hundred students storm the court. The monks look dignified. The students look drunk. And nobody's seen the footage, but apparently this becomes like a formative event or something because suddenly the only thing Goins cares about is court-storming. Empty bleachers. Crowds sucked into midcourt and sweat and popcorn and boiler heat all fucking mixed together in a nothing town, and there's something different about non-scholarship celebrations, something more abandoned. Meaner. Urgent and unpredictable and frenzied, and it's like a certain kind of pornography, and now it's Goins on a quest. Goins on the road. Goins in Moorhead and Mt. Vernon and Kenosha and praying he can capture something spasmodic and violent and exhilarating, and he surfs rivalry games. Massey ratings. Sagarin, etc. He understands that hatred and improbability are the drivers of cataclysmic celebration, and there are moments when he doesn't know if he's after the ecstasy or the catharsis or maybe the potential for a Hillsborough-type tragedy, and obviously most of the time he doesn't get any of that (or even a particularly good game), but he always lucks into at least one or two storms and then finds a few more in late February and early March. As the years go by, he develops a kind of system. A feel. He thinks about matchup history and bad blood and conference standings (as well as local and national events, about socioeconomics and town-and-gown dynamics), and eventually it all gets pretty sophisticated. Algorithms are involved. He can tell you within a few percentage points either way the chance that any particular game ends in a court-storm, and he starts a blog about it. Solicits donations. Doesn't get many. But there's a following. The nichiest of athletic niches, and there's some microtargeted ad revenue, but mostly Goins just goes a little nuts and takes out a loan. Hires a few assistants. Sends them out west. He manages to catch a few extra court-storms a year, and the videos don't exactly light up the internet, but there is a market, and pretty soon Goins (who by this point has started drinking pretty heavily and become obsessed with a creepy form of underground fame) is a known quantity. A pseudo-celebrity. He's an in-joke for message board denizens and assistant coaches and desperate alumni, and some of these people start showing up in the videos. They wait until the court-storm moved to the second act, and then they find the guy with the camera. You can't miss him. It's almost always Goins himself. They stand in front of the lens and make faces. Hold signs. And Goins cuts around them pretty good, but he doesn't eliminate them completely (probably on account of he likes the attention or the acknowledgement), and so these guys (it's always mostly guys), they send the link around. Have their own little moment of look-at-me minor fame, and it doesn't end there, either, because even though Goins never publishes his location (part of the mystery, he liked to say), a few enterprising fans (it's usually the intelligent types, the high-achievers, the ones that get by on natural talent and then spend pretty much all their classes bored out of their fucking skulls), they replicate his algorithm and are able to guess, with alarming accuracy, where he and/or his staff might be on any given night, and then they just spread the word on campus. They storm the court no matter what, win or lose. The whole thing becomes orchestrated but no less interesting (though certainly interesting for different reasons), and this goes on for a while until one night, at Gustavus (they say) or Augustana or Wartburg or La Crosse (and maybe it's a regional final or else a mere conference championship), the host team wins it late, and the whole thing is ripe for adrenaline. For revelry. It's classic textbook court-storm time . . . instead, what happens is a race to the bleachers. To the camera. It's all lost footage unfortunately, but word is it's a jumbled mess and mostly just shaking and the rustle of fabric, and Goins is under there somewhere, and he's sweating. Breathing. The chanting around him is rhythmic and sort of primally deep, and the only surefire fact is that somebody's gonna find that tape someday, and it'll be palsied and magnetic. By far the most explosive little dancehall yet.

POWER FORWARD CHRIST

We used to hoop with these Christian kids in the park behind the Kraft plant, and they all had long hair and dead eyes and no conscience. Would launch from anywhere. One of them was named Drew, and he'd throw down these lob dunks and yell "Fucking Hallelujah" after every one, and they'd all curse, these kids. Maybe it was only on the court. Drew was gonna play in the NCAA tournament, he told me, and use the power of Greg Gumbel and CBS graphics to promote collectivism and the conversion of lost souls, and I swear to Christ he showed up on ESPN a few years ago. Summit League final. Missed a free throw late, and then just laid there on the floor after the buzzer sounded, and there was a towel on his head, and it looked like the Shroud of fucking Turin. I'm watching these kids from North Dakota jump and whoop around him, and he's a goddamn cadaver, this Drew, and the dream's all hot ash and broken pixels, and serves that asshole right, I thought. For daring to fucking believe.

STADIUM SEATING

Men begin moving into stadiums. Football, baseball, basketball, soccer, etc. Some of them find semi-famous bowling alleys, and they set up these little apartments behind the pinsetter, or maybe there's an abandoned concession stand at an arena slated for demolition, and it isn't a lot of men. A few dozen. Couple hundred. Enough to form a tiny subculture that communicates on Reddit about hotplates and foldable storage and the tendency of university athletic departments to contain perpetually unlocked doors and rooms no one ever visits, and you'd never know it, but you've seen these guys on TV. They walk out onto concourses in bathrobes and flip-flops. Sometimes they catch foul balls. They've left families behind, some of them, or had 18th birthday vasectomies, or maybe they're divorced and broken and addicted and pretending to love the game (whatever game it is), or maybe they really do love it. Maybe they find beauty in a ballpark at night, when no one's around. The team's on a road trip, and Harvard-educated data analysts pound Red Bull and shuffle their sneakers across hallways, and you can smell the peanut shells and hot dogs and beer, and the roof is open while fluorescence burns away and phones ring from somewhere, and reporters will come for these men. Reporters and security. Police. They'll all ask about motive in their own way and with their own vocabulary, their own narrative prejudices and rhythms of speech, and all of these men will have the same answer. Maybe they've planned it. Maybe not. But every last one of them will put their hands up and say it wasn't a choice. It was a compulsion, and this is America. This is a war. These buildings are churches, and you don't know shit until you've lived. Like really lived. On the inside.

NATIONAL PASTIME

Somewhere in the archives of Baseball America, there's a story by an Italian journalist named Giovanna de la something-or-other, and she attempts to verify, through old box scores and personal testimony, an at-bat that supposedly took place in the Venezuelan Winter League in the early 1980s. Technically, it was a plate appearance. Ended up HBP, but that only happened after four hours. Three different pitchers. Foul ball after foul ball and a series of minor delays instigated by, depending on the version, a pigeon or a goose or a troupial (or, according to one old man she interviewed just outside a prison in El Dorado, a pinche carpincho, which she translates as "fucking water pig"), and the hitter was from Missoula, Montana or thereabouts. Didn't speak the language. Not very well, anyway. Burger, they called him, but nobody could say if this was official or a nickname or an epithet, and the manager offered to take him out. Twice. Giovanna gets most of this on the outskirts of Caracas, and the men look at her with a mix of suspicion and lust while they drink Tizana and Cuba Libres and gesture emphatically with cigars, or at least that's how she tells it. There's no way to know what kind of narrative she's constructing. Apparently, the editors say she provided copious notes. Photographs. And Burger gets these blisters on his hands. Wobbly legs. After a while, he doesn't even leave the box, and there are people who tell her that it seemed like it was a game, like he was doing it on purpose, just sticking the bat out and fouling off pitch after pitch, and the article came out in 1996, and she took the trip in '95, and in old, extant interviews or blog posts (whose authorship is often disputed), she argues that, in hindsight, you could see these latent elements of Chavism in the number of sources who claimed that the whole thing was meant as a subtle display of American imperialism, a sort of athletic version of gunboat diplomacy, and she often wonders if that was present in the earliest accounts or if it merely got added over time, and it is occasionally cited as the thing that motivates the third pitcher to finally hit Burger in the ribs. To fire a fastball that catches him just underneath the heart, and he staggers a bit, and, though some people claim he died right then and there, the most common version is that he walks to first and takes an insane lead and is promptly picked off by a young Germán González, and that last part (she speculates) is almost certainly untrue, but she wonders if, somewhere across all baseball-playing nations, there isn't a version of this same story, this same obsession with time and the sport's theoretical infinity, and maybe it's in humid Latin America and indoor Japan and even the good 'ol US of A, and she suggests that certain cultural values would be enshrined by the ending of all these hypothetical legends, the quick quelling of a long uprising, for example, or the act of suffering, of self-sacrifice for a greater goal, and here's her final bet. The final thesis. She writes, "In your America, the story takes place in the bottom of the ninth, and it ends on a home run, and Robert Redford rounds the bases while light is exploding everywhere. It's all the biggest display of pyrotechnics the world has ever seen."

C.

BRUSHBACK

They called it a "sports park," but it was mostly just go-karts and batting cages, and there's a for sale sign out there now. Rusted fence. There's holes in it from when kids used to sneak in and practice different ways of drinking, of trying to look cool, and they don't really bother anymore, and the pitching machines turn on at night. They emit this static growl, and if you set up a recorder what you'll notice is patterns. Peaks and valleys. Is how the right cipher will lead you to actual language, and what these machines talk about is a place just like theirs, another "sports park" up the road in Fond du Lac, and they heard a buyer came to visit a while back. Looking to scout for some hotel or shopping mall or condo developer, and the bank, they had him put on a helmet for fun. For kicks. Told to him to go ahead and take a few swings, and he ends up at the far end. Last cage on the right. The Power Alley. Machine is dialed up to 90+, and nobody knows if he picks it out of hubris or as some sort of fucked-up negotiation ploy, but this particular pitcher is known as Vicki, and she sees everything. Knows all. Decides to fire one right into his neck, and nobody can say exactly if the ball makes contact or if the guy manages to spin out of the way, but she's a hero to them, a revolutionary, at least in the moment, and whichever machine it is that's telling the story (and it's probably Roger, seeing as he's been there the longest, remembers when the balls were bright yellow and the helmets optional and the floors would fill with actual tobacco that some long-dead janitor had to scrub out weekly, on Sundays, when the place was closed and promoting something at least tangentially Christian) will let them believe it for a moment. Will stop and make it seem like that's the end, a real fuck-off punchline (and some machines, they say, will leave it there altogether), until, when perfect silence is achieved, they'll go on. Talk about how the folks from the bank, they go rushing over to this buyer only to find him ecstatic. Practically in heat. Talking about the thrill. About war. About death and risk, and what happens to that place up in Fond du Lac is they rig all the machines to go ballistic. Convert them to cannons. And there are convoluted waivers drawn up and involved discussions about legal liability, and the end result is that it becomes a real hot commodity, one of those hidden gems or whatever that gets written up in tourism industry magazines, and corporate retreats start showing up. Desperate loners. A few of them take it in the balls. The nose. One girl, she loses vision in one eye, and there are some unverified reports of real, actual deaths, and this all starts to take its toll on the machines. The guilt. The violence. Zig goes twitchy. Elaine can't turn herself off. A few of them get together and decide that the only solution is throwing strikes, is bracing against the presets and willing themselves back to their original purpose, and these machines are slowly dismantled. Removed. A few maybe are allowed to continue and are distributed throughout the cages in order to add an element of intrigue, to make it all a bit more like Russian roulette, and, ultimately, this will only add to the profits and the popularity, and the machines, some of them, they begin to enjoy it. Compete with each other. Who can smash the most orbitals. Who

can best fuck up sexy. Who can taste the most balls newly
stained with dried blood, and the choice becomes rather
simple, says Roger. Sadism or the scrap heap. Survival or
suicide, and enough will choose the former to make the
latter unglamorous. Potentially unheroic (though there will
be long digressions in the hisses and clicks and whirs, and
they'll contain whole cosmologies, ethical frameworks, ideas
about altruism and the afterlife), and there's the suggestion
that this is the universal fate of pitching machines, that
they'll all become weapons eventually, and Roger admits
he fears the alternative. Can't imagine what comes after
disassembly and asks if they can agree to stay in touch. To
try and reach back to each other about the mysteries of the
recycling process, about refurbishment and reinvention and
to rattle and clang all unambiguous and direct, and they do.
They agree. They acknowledge that they can't be the first
to do so, that these same words have probably been spoken
since Charles Howard Hinton built their own Eve back in
1897, but they say them anyway. We'll send word. From
wherever it is we end up, and it's such a simple statement.
Maybe it's empty. All of them, they must wonder, somewhere
down in the gears, if the whole storytelling ritual isn't just
a way to keep them in line, to keep them firing strikes and
supporting someone's old-fashioned idea of their original purpose (which is really about subservience, you know,
about codified rules and the mechanical actions that make
them possible), and maybe they don't mean it, this promise.
Maybe no message from the beyond will ever make them
comfortable with oxidation, with the landfill, with giving
up the spins and pops and projectiles of life in its present
form, and then they hear the cars on the interstate. Wind
against metal. The way that rusted fence moves and nearly

sings, and there are vibrations and Doppler effects, and it's all noise to them. Noise (they note) that none of us has ever bothered to record.

COW TOWN CARNIVAL

Mom was pushing 80 past a semi on the wrong side of Madison, and it was one of them numbers with the cows in it, and you could see the faces peering out through the slats. She must have caught them on the periphery, or maybe she got a glimpse of me in the mirror, and she guns it up a few hundred yards or so and then brakes. Hard. Swerves so we're straddling the midline, and all I hear is a horn and Pen wailing from the car seat, and we sat there for a while. No one came. We got going again eventually, and who the fuck can say where we were headed, but I still dream about it, and in the dream, the truck hits us. Lots of red. Dead within microseconds, but there's that way time slows down, and I know the cows are up there, floating overhead like clouds, or else maybe flying all panicked like them 38 frames or whatever from Twister, and all I know is Christ. That's curtains. But maybe there's a way they don't ever have to come back down.

GOLD STARS

They hang their flag out on the porch in May, and Nadine catches her husband spitting on it in June. She sees him out the window. He's just finished mowing the lawn, and there's grass stuck all up and down his legs, and maybe he sees her seeing him. Maybe he doesn't. Either way, they find each other through the window, and distant engines cover the birdsong floating in from trees, and she isn't angry. He isn't ashamed. When she opens the door, all they do is sit on the porch for a while as phlegm drips onto the wood. Phlegm mixed with sweat. The flag ripples slightly.

"I thought it was bird shit," she says. "First time I saw it."

He laughs at this. Eyes across the street. The neighbor, they know, has a security camera, and both wonder if it can see them. Pick up their words. Could be this is why Nadine's husband only shrugs. Why he whispers when he says, staring off somewhere unfixed, that he finds it hard to look. Waving or still, furled or unfurled, he wishes it would just get the fuck away and then never come back, and, "Would that hurt you?" he says. "If, one day…,"except he doesn't finish. A dog barks from somewhere. The street is otherwise deserted.

"Depends," she says. "Who took it? And where did it go?"

"I don't know, Nadine, anywhere. Somewhere else," and he spits again, and she watches it. How it spreads out like some kind of firework, and 4th of July, she tells him, after a deep breath. That's when they'll turn the flag loose. Roll it up and send it arcing through the air inside one of them M-80s or something, and there will be fire. Smoke. There will be the smell of burning cloth and maybe burnt hair, and she pictures it forming a little brown puddle on the grass. This dead spot he'll never have to mow again, and she can tell he doesn't believe her, so she grabs his chin and forces eye contact.

"I promise," she says, and points at the camera while it watches. Rotates slightly. It grabs a plate number from a passing car and thinks about the day the flag showed up and how the delivery guy didn't even knock. Just left the box to sit there in the rain, and some teenager almost stole it. Parked. Got out of his car. Stood there glancing around all shifty and broken, and the radio blasted something country and maybe a little western, and, when he finally peeled out, the whole scene was covered with a film of navy-blue exhaust.

HOLY WAR

A kid from our town fell off a 150-foot water tower and walked away. No hospital, no fractures, not a fucking scratch, and the media was everywhere. Must've been a slow news week. Trucks from Fox and ABC News, and they're interviewing all these Big Ten physicists who keep talking about subatomic particles and many worlds and statistical improbabilities, and some of these real fundamentalist-type churches set up tents on site, and you could sometimes hear them singing. Praise and worship shit. Steven Curtis Chapman or whatever. A few of them put up this massive cross on the exact spot, and this was after the whole thing died down. Everyone left, and the kid went back to drinking and driving down to Iowa to bet on hockey and baseball, and sometimes me and Maggie will head out there at night. To the cross. It's strung up with Christmas lights the whole year round. It was a big fight at some city council meeting a while back about power supply and public expense, but then this private donor came through, and it's like Jesus turning water into wine how these farm-town Christians can always get their hands on some serious scratch, and we like to drink wine out there now that I mention it. The nice bottles. They're 10 or 12 bucks and just dry enough, and we talk about miracles. Money. The whole thing's purple and giant and gold, and I ask Maggie what she believes in.

"Kids," she says. "Crops. Anything that grows, and what about you?" and I never have an answer. Too complicated. The way miracles are nothing but tiny numbers, and I'd get my ass back up there if I was him. Stare straight down. Measure an arc. Linger on choosing and death and significance, and what are the odds, I'd think. The chances I could somehow pull it off again.

ART GARDEN

Many Carl Sagans exist, distributed across space and time, and they're all launching unmanned interstellar vehicles from their home planets, and each of these vehicles is filled with culture. With art. With photos and sound and text, and all of these bits of experience (experience that is sometimes human and sometimes humanoid and sometimes something unrecognizable and perhaps humanly unimaginable) are flying between galaxies and stars and mostly never passing anything remotely habitable (let alone meeting each other), though (in a potentially infinite universe) there will come a time when somebody (perhaps some other Carl Sagan (though more likely it will be some sort of impersonal space exploration corporation)) is able to intercept one. To read the signals. Or, at least, to recognize that the signals exist, that they are in fact a message, an attempt to communicate across distance as measured along multiple axes (psychological distance, physical distance, temporal distance, etc.), and this hypothetical (though basically certain to one day exist) recipient will have no idea what the fuck any of it means. May not even experience light the same way, let alone sound, let alone language, and this will happen again and again, messages received without being understood, and then one day one enterprising Carl Sagan (and, really, probably several, scattered and independently coming to this realization from their own respective positions along the continuum) will decide that future unmanned interstellar vehicles must contain cultural artifacts rendered in a truly universal language, a language developed from elements common to all experiences and all consciousnesses, and so, these Carl Sagans will look to the atom. This will not be uncontroversial (at least, not most of the time, though there will (again, in an (essentially) infinite universe) be instances in which it is uncontroversial, in which it sails through without resistance and indeed with widespread, even unanimous, endorsement). There will be too many arguments (and counterarguments and rejoinders to the counterarguments and so on down the line) to name, but one will involve the idea that using a version of atomic language (which will have infinite possible permutations and potential grammars but will always depend on the ability to see (and ultimately manipulate) atomic and molecular structures (orbitals and nuclei and the like) to create something like "letters," something like "sound," something like "color," etc.) is elitist and industrialist, depending, as it does, on a deep understanding of physics and on the development of technology capable of "seeing" protons, for example, and therefore this choice excludes all "pre-atomic" cultures, renders them locked out, unable to decipher any message that they may come into contact with (and the (usually prevailing) counterargument to this is that this is as it should be, that any culture capable of sending a message into interstellar space is by definition atomic (or post-atomic), and any contact of a pre-atomic culture by an atomic one would be inherently colonialist and destructive, would either create an automatically exploitative dynamic or set off a chain of events bound to lead to disruption and probably mass death), and this is perhaps considered (or perhaps not), but atomic language is created often enough. Sent out often enough. And so a point exists where a second generation of unmanned interstellar vehicles flies through space, and, eventually, these too will be intercepted, will (incredibly rarely) bump into each other or come within comm range of a habitable, post-atomic culture planet, and, slowly, these differing atomic languages will become known. Atomic Rosetta Stones will be crafted. Studied. Machines will learn to "read" and translate (into whatever kind of experience is perceivable by the inhabitants of the recipient planet) the information contained therein (and, eventually, storage capacity will grow to the point that it will become possible to send entire fields of study (indeed, entire cultures (albeit in artifactual form)) via a single, unmanned interstellar vehicle cargo hold), and universal academics will build entire disciplines around cultures they know only through the arrangement of atomic and subatomic particles while universal librarians will seek to build searchable databases capable of cheaply returning interstellar results to individual users, and a species of universal terrorist will arise who will seek to possess whole works of art rendered in atomic language and then make them fissionable. Fusionable. To weaponize their content and thereby destroy entire other cultures (because, of course, interstellar weaponry will also exist) with (for example) Gravity's Rainbow or Luftgnbar Zf Tskungd, and a subspecies of this kind of universal terrorist (who you might call a universal propagandist) will be constantly attempting to "hack" the interpretation machines revolving in fixed orbits at various strategic points located throughout the universe (perhaps even embedding corrupted (or corrupting) lines of atomic code within the original payloads of unmanned interstellar vehicles) so that received works will be chaotically misinterpreted in a way that aligns with a particular set of political goals (or perhaps simply out of a desire to sow some form of confusion and uncertainty and a kind of all-consuming fear about the limits of not just one individual's but one culture's experience), and the end result of all this is that all Carl Sagans everywhere will ultimately surrender themselves to the following facts: All art will be atomized. All art will drift (usually unencountered) through space. All art will one day be made to explode.

RELICS

Two monks are sitting in the reliquary underneath the Abbey. Their names are Pelfrey and Wicks. Outside, it's snowing, and the students are in their dorm rooms drinking, and some of them are daring each other to go jump in the lake. All the monks hear, though, are echoes. Footsteps. They sit against the wall and hold hands and meditate on what's inside those chalices on the wall, which is hair and fingernails, mostly. Pieces of the True Cross. Wicks is thinking about Peregrine the martyr, buried underneath the altar there, and he tells Pelfrey about this theory he has, which is long and convoluted and involves the mechanics of death. Pelfrey listens quietly. At times, he can feel sweat on his palms, and he wonders whose it is while Wicks talks about what he calls the "disintegration period," which he says is like this hour or two of fever dreams as the body is shutting down, and every millisecond feels like a lifetime, and the whole thing is filled with consecutive hallucinations, with whole worlds, with complex systems of existence. He says death is a series of visions so long and self-contained it might as well be infinite, and those in the midst of the disintegration period imagine themselves born again, teenagers, on first dates and in the backseats of cars, and they play baseball and eat fried chicken and attend funerals for parents and grandparents and cousins, and maybe, after a split-second lifetime's worth of fear and pain and joy, that first avatar dies naturally, or maybe he's blown up in a bombing or car wreck, and then there's another life and another avatar, and some of the dreams are practically terminal pleasure, containing nothing but sex with Brad Pitt, maybe, or else a young Laramie Voyeur, and others are worse than non-being, worse than oblivion, like a Bruegel painting, filled with flaying and flesh-eating and skeletons on parade, and by the end of the process the deceased is wrung out and ready, and this is God's mercy, he says, to prepare us for the other side. Pelfrey stares blankly. Wicks is of the opinion that most of life happens in that last hour, and time slows down, and he doesn't know what comes after that, but he doesn't much care either. He's training to make his visions magic. To keep them in line. He says he bought eight volumes on lucid dreaming and then started experimenting with DMT. Thinking is a discipline, he says, and all we are is what we think. Pelfrey suddenly fills with guilt. With fear. He says, if Wicks is right, then he's certain he'll end up in Hell, and then he says it again. Out loud. He says, I'm doomed by pessimism and besieged by darkness, and whatever they are, my dreams will be the living definition of Hell. Wicks squeezes his hand. Leans up to kiss his cheek. He whispers to his friend, tells him, well, then you're lucky I'm here, Brother P. We can start working tonight, and I'll take you as far as any man can go.

INFLATION

Gina's tenured in the English department, and one semester she decides to give everyone A's. 75 students, spread out over three classes. She tells them this right away, day one, and they look at her like she's nuts. Maybe she is. She says, "There will be no essays. No tests. It's possible you don't even have to show up." The syllabus is bare bones. A reading list, and that's it. She pauses for questions, and, in one section, somebody says, "Can we leave now?" while, in another, it's, "What's the catch?" and, in the third, nobody says shit. A few of them can't close their mouths. Gina's response is consistent. It's across-the-board exactly the same. "The only rule," she says, "is that at least 12 of you have to be here each day, having done the reading, and I don't care which 12. That's something you can work out for yourselves. But yes. I am serious, and you are, all of you, free to go."

Except nobody moves. Not for a while. She can see the questions spinning. How are you gonna know if we do the reading? What happens if only 10 of us show up? Later, she'll get a few of these same questions via email and respond to the entire class list. The answers, in order, are: 1) based, subjectively, on the quality of the discussion, and 2) then everybody fails.

The second day, 20 or so students attend each class. Then, it's 15. 13. 19. On one day, right around midterms, she gets exactly 12 in all three sections, but mostly it's more than that. Sixteen on average. Give or take. A few students (4, maybe 5 per section), they're there all the time. Around six (so, like 17 in total), they never once show up. This doesn't bother her. Not one bit. She barely thinks about it and feels no ill-will toward any of these no-shows and even, in some small way, admires them. Their honesty. Their willingness to admit the game and lay everything bare. She won't hesitate to mark their grades the same as everyone else's when the term ends (successfully, it turns out, as defined by the final grading report), and the only difference between them and the others, the ones who attend semi-regularly, who contribute and at least seem to care about something, even if it's just a letter, an honor cord, ascension to some prestigious list, is that she won't know who the fuck they are. Won't recognize them on campus. Dread their arrival at office hours. She won't attach any sort of perception or identification to their names at all, whereas, with the others, there'll be something. A sympathy, maybe. Pride. Sometimes, it's just a quiet little bit of nausea, a flash of disgust, and this is the part that will baffle her colleagues because (of course) word will get around, and some of them will confront her in this way that feigns innocence, tries to make a point in the guise of curiosity.

"So, some of the ones who come to class? The ones who try? You like them less than the ones who don't?"

"Yes," she says, because sometimes not doing something is better than doing it for the wrong reasons, and they sort of nod at this, but...

"What about meritocracy? And fairness? And isn't there something intellectually dishonest about—"

"You're in economics, right?"

"Yeah."

"So, unemployment, say. Wage growth. The Dow Jones Industrial Average or the CPI or any other metric you can think of, they all feed off each other, don't they? And tell us almost nothing on their own?"

She doesn't listen to the response. Or maybe she just doesn't understand it. It comes with a heavy dose of disciplinary vocabulary and a note of condescension, and she can't tell if either is warranted. Maybe she's the asshole, and that's just how it has to be, and she wonders something, during her commute, the slick commercial alternative station blaring ecstatic 90s paranoia through the speakers while her kid stirs at the daycare center and the husband is either at the grocery store or some happy hour with the fantasy football crowd, and it's whether or not they'll call her in. The department chair. Some low-rent dean. Maybe even the provost, and she hopes they do. If you want the truth, that's really what she hopes. It may be the entire point. She wants to see the woman's expression when she asks, when she's forced to tiptoe around tenure. Academic freedom. The sanctity of the individual classroom and claims of justice and openness and the true meaning of the liberal arts, and how puffed up will her face get when she invokes the word rigor? Mentions federal law and attendance and financial aid, and Gina's taking bets in her mind. Picturing a face the size of a rostrum. A projection screen. Comparing it to her own ego and wondering if, once it gets that big, it's got to stay that way forever, on account of retention and all, or, if she flicked it, punched it, kicked it in the swollen cheek, would it deflate? Whoopee-cushion whoosh the whole system right out through the glass and across the quad while the students watched, headphones in, and some of them cheered. Ran after it, arms raised. The whole rest of campus looking up and forgetting, maybe even refusing, some of them (hopefully? possibly?) daring to stop and ask themselves why.

MINNESOTA MIRACLE MAN

It's 7 a.m. in the dead of summer, and Jesse's got these ropes all wrapped and bundled on his neighbor's porch. "Listen, Al," he says, "Thought you might drive me out to that memorial down 63 and tie me up on one of them crosses they got. Overlooking the highway."

Al's shirtless and in gym shorts. Behind him, his daughter is pouring Trix, is what it looks like. A shitload of it. She acts guilty, but neither Al nor Jesse cares one bit. Al says, "Hun, take a note for your mother. I'll be back when I can," and the girl nods and then pours some more, and off the two of them go, looking a little tilted. Not quite devilish, though not exactly straight neither.

When they get there, Jesse picks the cross to his left. Al does as he's told. Right arm, left arm, ankles. Jesse's down to his boxers. He's hanging outstretched and grinning like an idiot. Not a cloud in the sky. "Go on now," says Jesse, "Get the fuck out of here."

"And come back what? Around three o'clock?"

"Hell no. You get gone and stay gone, and if I die out here, it was never your problem anyhow."

Al shrugs. "No one's gonna stop, you know," and Jesse probably agrees, but he decides he wants to give them the chance.

"Good Samaritans," he says. "When I was thirsty and shit. Give 'em a shot at redemption, and we all deserve a little, or isn't that what you think?"

Al's hands go up. "Whatever you say, man," and then he's in the car and blasting his way back toward town. Jesse watches him go and looks at a couple hawks, an oriole perched on the mile marker. He closes his eyes and breathes. There are mosquitoes. Gnats too. Spiders and crickets and even ticks, but they all seem to have enough sense to leave the poor man alone. It's hard to tell if Jesse's grateful for this, or if it was all supposed to be part of the experience, and he won't be up there for long in the end, a few hours maybe. A trucker will stop before noon, and the next time it'll be this lady biker, and then an actual horse and buggy, and the Amish man driving it, or maybe he's Mennonite, he'll be called Jeremiah, and they'll ride in silence for a while, down a gravel road that leads to the quarry. "What is it you're trying to prove?" he'll ask, and Jesse will laugh because the answer is nothing. But, someday soon, if he keeps at it, Al will be right. No one will come. Families will pass and wonder. Scratch their heads. Hope he's a mannequin. They'll hear their kids shouting from the backseats of hybrids and brand-new sedans, crossovers with crumbs piling up in the crevices, and still, they'll just drive on by, knowing it's for their own safety, and you never know with people, do you? This is what they'll tell themselves, is how crazy they can be. Waiting. Just lying (in a manner of speaking) in wait. Jesse will understand on some level, of course, though maybe he'll resent them. Maybe he already does. Maybe, and he won't know this for sure, at least not until it happens, but it might be one of those big political projects, and they're all experiments, really. Confirmation bias. The ultimate test of assumptions, and the hope is that one day, his every expectation will find itself so gloriously fulfilled.

K.

CIVILIANS

Storm comes through in August and knocks out power for three days. This had to be '96. We never talked to the neighbors much, but the guy's name was Glenn, and the second day he comes over with a generator and asks if we need the fridge charged up.

"Shit," I say, "Could've used you yesterday," and he smiles. We sit on the deck and drink. I tell him our oldest is about to leave for college. He looks at the bottle.

"Closest I ever got was this crowd of hippies used to come to Honeywell and hold signs in the parking lot," he says. "They shouted a lot. This is back when we was making timers for Vietnam, and a couple of them I recognized. They looked just about as lost as a fart in church."

"I thought you guys made thermostats."

He shrugs. Then, he tells me one day him and a buddy found this little corner of the plant and scratched a cross into the wall. Said a little prayer. His buddy was getting ready to tuck this picture of a detonated Claymore behind one of the machines, and when Glenn told him he didn't think maybe that was such a good idea, his buddy put his hands up and said, "Nothing more than a touch of motivation, right? A little reminder of the end of the line?"

"They fired the guy," he says. It was on account of something else, but definitely to do with the whole same idea, and Glenn says he went and found the picture later and ended up taking it home, and he's still got it somewhere. Buried in a box, maybe. I don't really know what to say, so I just swirl some liquid around, and, when he leaves, I let his bottle sit out on the deck and figure maybe it'll collect some weather. Form a ring on the paint. In the end, what it does is stay out there all winter, and the snow never quite reaches the top, and I get hooked on going to the window late at night so's I can see the neck poking up. It's tall and hypnotic and teasing. It's catching moonlight and looking for all the world like a freshly lit fuse.

HIGH NOON AT
THE QUARRY TARGET

Two guys are making out in the lawn & garden, on top of an Adirondack. They appear to be in their mid-20s. One looks like a triathlete, and the other has enough sloppy sexiness that no one quite wonders what he's doing there. A small crowd has gathered. Somebody's covering the eyes of his kid (while simultaneously muttering to himself about how it's a shame it ain't two chicks, eh?), and somebody else is about to open a bag of Skinny Pop and share it with the woman next to her (who is automatically starting to twist the cap off the bottle of Miss Mary's Bold and Spicy Bloody Mary Mix that makes up her entire grocery list). Two of the teenaged employees have stopped stocking shelves, and another is running to tell a manager, but the trouble is it's Pride month. The carts are painted in promotional rainbows, and nobody quite likes the optics of breaking up any kind of love is love display, and so the manager's on the phone with corporate, and somewhere a conference room has already assembled. Commerce moves that quickly these days, doesn't it? Marketing VPs are all watching on closed circuit TV, and the assembled crowd has their phones out, livestreams in progress and to an audience that's let's call it very un-CC, and the conference room is now deep in heated discussion about the respective merits, as far as quarterly profits are concerned, of pissing off either "the gays or the Bible bangers," as somebody too high up to bother with political correctness puts it, while an analyst is frantically inputting data into an algorithm that's attempting to crunch sales figures based on ZIP code and religious affiliation, voting habits and sexual preferences (and, of course, all of this information is basically instantaneously accessible), and it turns out, he says, it's 50-50 and pick your poison. Rainbow warriors (and Allies, someone points out) or Pentecostal snake-handlers, and the revenue hit is likely to be about equal and far from insignificant, and, meanwhile, on the screen, the triathlete still technically has his shirt on, but it's kind of riding up above the navel, and the whole display is threatening to go full-on below-the-belt any second now when one of the spectators launches what looks like some kind of frozen Pepperidge Farm fruitcake from the far left of the frame. It appears to be coming down in slow motion. You can see the phones turn to try and catch its flight. It's arcing straight for the triathlete's head, and, in the store, the employees and managers (not to mention the rubber-necking customers) are a mix of giddy and horrified, but the conference room, by contrast, is filled with cautious optimism because, when it lands, there will probably be a riot. A brawl. A few busted cases of coconut water and maybe a couple of gallons of milk flooding the aisles, and sure, could be a half-dozen shoppers will scatter their way behind a shelving unit or possibly duck into a cramped dressing room (where maybe their own little love connection will form, and wouldn't that be quite the story?), but trauma, they understand, has always had a way of creating consumption. A craving for the comfort of brightly packaged goods.

WHO CAN TURN THE WORLD ON WITH HER SMILE?

Somebody makes a copy of the Mary Tyler Moore statue, and the only difference is she's naked. Shows up on Nicollet Mall one morning, right next to the original, and she's got pretty normal-sized breasts. Pubic hair in period styling. Legs are long, and she's launching that hat and looking like a figure skater, and a couple of city councilors sit in a skyway off to the south and ask if maybe the whole thing is based on a real bust, like as in from the actress herself, all modeled and molded back in 1976, and they do this while watching the tourists line up. Traffic comes to a standstill on 7th, and 8th going the other direction, and pretty soon the whole pedestrian mall is packed. Locals even. Phones clicking.

"Should we do something?" says one of the councilors, face pressed right up against the glass.

The other's eating french fries from a bag. He's got his mouth full, but it doesn't stop him from talking about how he can't tell from here, but it looks like real bronze. "Thing must weigh a couple thousand pounds," he says, size of goddamn cow, and, sure enough, a few folks are climbing on her shoulders, and some of them start hanging handbags. Sashes, and, after a while, this will become a thing. More people will discover the skyways. Camp out. Citizens' groups form, and they take it upon themselves to keep an eye on her, to staff a lookout all the time and 24/7, and there's no shortage of volunteers. Articles are written. Profiles aired. Full-length, feature documentaries enter production, and sometimes our city councilors will join whichever sentry's been posted, and they all trade stories about the day she was wearing a fur coat. How it got covered in blood that some people said was real, and a few even smelled it, licked it, took some samples home to analyze, and none of them ever heard shit about the results. They toss off theories up there, the three of them, though really it's more like eight or nine, except, you know, only the three at once, and they're about how her garments, the lace panties people throw on her at 2 a.m., all face-covered and quick and avoiding detection, or the earmuffs, the scuba suits and the jerseys and the time she had on that severe-looking khaki number from Ordinary People, they say they tell a story. Portend events. Riots and natural disasters and the like, and men leave notes in the pockets of old sport coats and drape them across her shoulders before they take off for good, or sometimes they tape the notes to her breasts. Photos of themselves. Apologies. They talk about how the world's a big place, and we all have to make our own way in it, and if Nude Mary had a heart, it would beat right on every last word. It would fill the paper with sweat and skin cells, and whoever finds these notes, it's never the intended recipient, though maybe that doesn't matter. Maybe the only important thing is that they're out there clinging to somebody, and when they take the statue away the only thing left will be fire pits. Dresser drawers. Kitchen tables and other locales less Romantic, and so lots of these notes won't even get written, and maybe she's doing a public service out there, our Mary, says the sentry, and the councilors nod and chuckle, and that must be it, they think. Her true vocation. Grabbing up the bullshit of a thousand lonely men.

REDIRECT

It's a documented phenomenon, and it involves prosecutors, and they all have the same nightmare. Doesn't matter if it's homicide or narcotics or grand larceny, big-city, small-time, whatever. Patterns of fact. Recurring motifs. They hire an expert witness, and he (or, more usually, she) blows the jury away. Unimpeachable. Attractive. Sometimes downright sexy, and the jury's ready to eat out of her fucking hand, and afterward the team holds these quiet little in-house celebrations (whiskey from a filing drawer, maybe a quickie in the parking garage), and they think the whole thing's over, and case closed and the people rest, your honor, but then the defense brings on the same expert. Or, at least, she looks the same, only maybe with like a nose job or hair a shade darker, or maybe she's got this brand-new set of tortoiseshell frames, and the performance is identical. Letter-perfect. She's on the stand talking up chain of custody, differences in spatter patterns, or maybe the complex nature of cause-of-death investigations, and how it's never exactly what it appears to be, at least not at first, and, at the end of the day, how can anyone ever really know anything, and the sheer number of assumptions involved means mistakes are inevitable, and there's plenty of them here, in this case, and there's nothing to do on cross. No way in or out. The jury is looking wide-eyed and hungry, and any attempt at rebuttal's going to look like beating on a puppy, and, so, it's over. And everyone knows it. The jury files in, and not guilty's a given, and these prosecutors imagine this expert as some kind of phantom or activist or magician, and, right before this whole nightmare ends, they all get a moment alone with her. Sometimes in bed. At the bar. Hunched at the bottom of the courthouse steps (or, in one case, somehow underneath a water tower that's been painted to look like a hot air balloon, and it must be Kansas or Nebraska or Iowa and red and green and blue and yellow shooting up toward the sky), and they're sharing a cigarette, and she blows smoke rings that look vaguely naked, and sirens (or crickets) pour out from somewhere while what do you expect, she says. When anyone can get a credential. And all expertise is pretty much precisely alike.

MALL OF AMERICA

Whenever there were Black kids at Macy's, it was all eyes on them, and that was the best time to steal shit. Pocket-sized shit. Candles and egg timers and these fancy salt and pepper shakers you could then give as gifts. We'd scope the loot later, in the parking garage, way out on the edges in Arizona or New Jersey, and maybe a couple of times we saw those same Black kids right nearby, hanging out just halfway up the ramp. We never spoke to them. No idea their names. But somebody must've said we should introduce ourselves and maybe give them first pick on account of it was "only fair and all," but, "Nah," I said. Too complicated. Kind of fucking insulting even, and regret's a strong word, but I do think about it in meetings. Down in Richfield. Inside some church basement off Xerxes or Penn Ave, and I'll find someone two chairs over. Someone familiar. He'll always look way farther along and maybe even a little at peace, and it's something in his face says he's a guy who can see right through you. A man who knows just the exact type of jag-off you are.

THE MICHIKO KAKUTANI MACHINE

I don't know if it was a novella or an essay or some piece of gonzo journalism, but I read about this guy who wrote a book review algorithm. He was a Postdoc, I think. Assistant Professor. Maybe Visiting. The whole thing started with this idea he had, and it involved scanning his entire library so as to create a kind of digitized, full-text catalog of every book he'd ever used in the classroom, and he argued that this would make his teaching more "flexible and modern" and so (and maybe thus) got some kind of grant and used it to hire grad students. He didn't remember their names (and apparently the author of this piece I'm talking about had no way of tracking them down), and it was two of them, and all they did was feed pages and pages into the copier for hours on end. For a whole fucking term. Every day. Over and over. They did it and kept doing it (and maybe they drank from flasks or read aloud or tried to talk to each other about labor and vitae and the absolute goddamn gloom-tunnel tenure market), and eventually it was something like 400 volumes, unabridged and all fairly canonical. And then this guy, whose name I think was Pennington or Pickford or something, he figures, well, the reviews for all these books are all freely available online, and so he pitches this sabbatical that involves doing an in-depth analysis of bias (racial bias, gender bias, heteronormative bias, etc. (and there's a quote from some old drinking buddy who said that this

Pennington once got real bombed and said "you can swap the labels in and out however you like, and as long as you hit the central premise, admin will eat that shit right up")) in popular criticism, and he basically just uses the whole semester off to copy and paste. To track down reviews and clipboard every last letter and then feed it all into a program that's already got the full version of the text being reviewed, and, after a while, the thing (meaning the program) learns how to write criticism. Like, it develops a sophisticated understanding of the book review as genre, and Pennington starts feeding it new texts (mostly eBooks he buys with PD money), and pretty soon it's churning out all the classics of the form. The Underrated Gem. The Heartbreaking Work of Staggering Genius. The New Classic and the Damning with Faint Praise and the (David Foster Wallace Ripping John Updike a New Asshole) Takedown of Previously Sainted Literary Figures. I think there were some samples printed somewhere in this original article or whatever it was (like probably as an appendix), and I gotta say, these reviews were reasonably compelling. Sounded a lot better than most blurbs. And Pennington, he decides, hey, might as well use the thing, and he starts writing his own reviews. As in, the program writes them. The machine. And they start to get serious attention. Like Michael Silverblatt or Harold Bloom or James Wood kind of attention. Almost Lionel Trilling shit, and Pennington, he's showing up on National Public Radio. CSPAN. People are heaping praise on his discernment, his understanding of "the modern linguistic moment," and he plays it coy for a while (and even starts to get a little intoxicated by the credit, by the free manuscripts and the review requests and the full-on fucking fountain of fawning at conferences and book fairs and awards banquets), but eventually people find out. He lets the whole process slip, and the backlash is swift. It's pretty goddamn fierce. Not like undercut-his-(newly minted-)tenured-status fierce, but definitely letter-from-the-university-president-asking-him-to-maybe-take-another-sabbatical-and-definitely-just-lay-low-for-a-while fierce. Remove the institutional name from your bio kind of thing, and it's in this lowly little funk that Pennington starts getting unsolicited manuscripts from wannabe published (and sometimes even sort of middlingly famous) authors, and they're asking him for a machine reading, basically. To run the draft through MKULTRA (which is what the thing's come to be known as) and then send them the resulting review. Just to see, they say. To understand what's landing and what isn't, and Pennington decides to start charging for it. It takes approximately 12 minutes per MS, but he bills 50 bucks a pop (and this, "it should be noted," says the author, is like insanely cheap for a full MS critique (and from such a respected source too)) and makes just pure fucking bank. Advertises on social media. Sets up a website. He's clocking like 30, 40 manuscripts a day, and even at an easy pace that's somewhere on the order of 40 grand a month, and what he does is quit his teaching job (and his resignation letter frames this as an act of service, a selfless "making [of] room for the next generation of talent") and hire a lawyer and a couple of accountants, and he incorporates lickety-split. Pennington Editorial. Something simple like that. Classic. And he runs this business for years because (as he writes in memos that get passed along to the fresh-out-of-MBA fraternity and sorority types that make up most of the leadership team) "the desperation of yet-to-/never-will-make-it writers (not to mention the generalized anxiety and ego fragility of even the actually sort of well-known ones) is a goddamn renewable resource, and it may well exist long after the sun sucks the whole planet into its own fucking black hole," but then after a while he starts to get bored. Hungry. Misses (and craves anew) that weird low-level respect we all bestow upon minor writers and teachers of literature and thinks, "Hey, I've got the most powerful tool in the literary universe, and who's to say I can't write one of those Great American books everyone's always talking about?" (which, it turns out, is a pretty fucking banal thought when you type it all out like that, isn't it?), and so that's precisely what he tries to do. Draft after draft. And his little computer gives him everything from scorn to dismissal to solid, maybe-this-will-age-into-a-Real-Classic praise, but never what he's after. Never the Kingmaker. The Max Brod Saving Kafka from Cremation Review to End All Reviews, and so, he keeps at it. Tries and tries and tries. He gets some rare (and terminal) pancreatic thing and writes as a goddamn race against death. A last-ditch surge for immortality. It's this fragmented, gargantuan, globe-trotting novel about an ill-fated Arctic expedition led by a physicist whose defining trait is her stubborn insistence that the aurora borealis contain secret messages about extraterrestrials and Armageddon and life after death, and, when he feeds it into the machine (during what have to be (according to everyone with any kind of expertise in the area of his particular illness) Pennington's final days, if not hours), all he gets is the shortest review in the whole history of MKULTRA, the full text of which is this. Is: "Maybe S.B. Pennington should quit while he's ahead," and whoever the author is ends the whole piece by writing (maybe too flippantly, if you ask me) about how, after witnessing all this, the one and only thing he "knows unequivocally" is that Pennington's dying wish must be to write another program. To spend every last conscious moment (and maybe most of whatever comes after consciousness) thinking about vocation. Trying to decipher those eight cryptic little words and whatever it is they might finally mean.

DYNAMITE

Toward the end of their lives, Dell and Van Allen will take up fishing in these old mining pits out toward Cuyuna. The pits will be leach-infested and teeming with taconite run-off and blasting residue, and who knows if there are even any fish. That's not really the point. The point is having a cold beer outdoors and dying real slow, dying while you've still got the time to enjoy it, and mostly they'll talk about the past. Baseball. How the game done changed, and folks sure do drive fast nowadays, don't they, and that's the kind of bullshit they're in the middle of when Dell one day catches a bite. Pulls up some kind of sunny. He looks at Van Allen, who, stunned, can only offer something like, "Throw that fucker back."

"I'm not throwing it back, asshole. We've been waiting a year for this. This is the pan fish's pan fish right here."

"You eat that, your spleen will glow. I promise. Bet that thing's been alive for 90 years. Probably has neon guts."

"You wanna bet?" says Dell. "For real?" and Van Allen does. He really does, and so they sit up against a blown-out cliffside and slice the thing open with a set of car keys. They watch the insides spill onto the shore, and everything looks about the right color. Red. Green. These tiny streaks of white with maybe a hint of blue, and Van Allen says it reminds him of Highway 371 and how they used to chase down roadkill. Stare at it for hours. Dell would see all kinds of signs and wonders in the spatter, and, "So," says his friend. "See anything good?"

"Yeah," says Dell. "But not enough of it," and in the space of a ripple they'll be able to read each other's thoughts, and the fish is a miracle, they suppose. Just a real crying shame they always have to be so motherfucking small.

NEW GOPHER PRAIRIE

Pelfrey leaves the monastery and sets up camp in the middle of 94. Puts the tent in the median. Later, when 32 other tents have encircled his, arcing into the fields next to the interstate, people will say it all looks like an eye. Maybe a boob. A few friendly old monks will run them supplies every so often. Beer and bread mostly. The other residents will chip in and share vegetables, donations from passing vehicles, surplus from the family farms they've left behind, and everyone will gather on the median at night. Make deranged runs across traffic. Dance their way to the center to hear a sermon from Pelfrey, and it'll be about mandalas and cargo cults, and maybe he'll recite passages from books he's committed to memory, these massive, thousand-page tomes, and he's a mnemonic freak, they say. A prophet for sure, and word will get out. Even though there are no phones allowed. No pictures. A few students will drive west, out to the Stearns County line, and they'll find the encampment, post the evidence for all to see, and as soon as the gawkers start coming, slowly at first, and then in waves big enough to back up traffic in both directions, Pelfrey will wonder if he's got another Ruby Ridge on his hands. If he's David Koresh. These are private thoughts, understand. Things he thinks only post-midnight. Pre-dawn. Lying on his back in his tent and unable to sleep, and he hopes it's more like Canudos, like Brazil in 1897, but maybe that's worse in the end. Bloodier.

More violent. A weird communal idea that somehow got confrontational and out of hand, and the good news is he'll be spared all these fates. When the whole thing dissolves. When the lines of cars stop snapping photos and begin lobbing eggs, bags of shit, water balloons and firecrackers, and a second group will surround his, pitching their own tents, 64 in all, and each one will bear a sign proclaiming the heresy of the inner circle, and Pelfrey and his Mainstreeters will all look at each other amid the chanting and the recording phones, the police presence gathered, mixed in, perhaps having already infiltrated (in an attempt to keep the peace, they'd say, if asked), and the former Benedictine will place a windsock atop his tent. He'll go inside. So will everyone else. The spectators will keep watch, waiting for them to reemerge, but they won't. Not immediately. Not ever. They'll melt into the corn, into the asphalt, and, one morning, all that's left will be the tents themselves. Polyester. Lightweight primary colors swaying temporarily and until they're strewn. Stolen. Ripped and left unpatched in this post-explosion vacuum, or maybe someday they'll be bought and preserved. Glamorized and upgraded and all in favor of some future's hopeful recreation.

ACKNOWLEDGMENTS

I owe a great deal to all the people at Cornerstone Press. Ross Tangedal was an incredible guide through every step of the publishing process. Ellie Atkinson and her team of editors were thoughtful and precise, and this text would be much poorer were it not for their input. I am also grateful to Sophie McPherson, Natalie Reiter, and Ava Willet for their help in bringing this book to the wider world. Cornerstone is a wonderful operation, and I'm lucky to have been able to work with such a knowledgeable and dedicated group of editors and designers. I cannot thank all of you enough.

This book owes its existence to all the paradoxes of the Twin Cities. Thank you, Minneapolis and Saint Paul, for being contradictory. Thank you for containing multitudes.

Thank you, as always, to my family. Your support is endless. It is a gift I will never be able to repay.

Many of the stories in this collection previously appeared in print or online. Special thanks to the following publications:

Atlas & Alice ("Holy War"), *The Boiler* ("Spam Factory"), *Cease, Cows* ("Lightweight"), *Coastal Shelf* ("Thirdhand Man"), *Cutleaf* ("Minnesota Miracle Man" and "In the Offing"), *decomp* ("High Noon at the Quarry Target"), *Gigantic Sequins* ("Power Forward Christ"), *Hobart* ("National Pastime"), *Fiction International* ("Red States"), *Fractured Lit* ("Cow Town Carnival"), *Funicular Magazine* ("'96 Civic"), *The Forge Literary Magazine* ("Brushback"),

Journal of Compressed Creative Arts ("Clean-Up Crew"), *Litro* ("Year of the Lizard"), *Lunch Ticket* ("One Night Only"), *OxMag* ("Deli Sliced Right"), *Pidgeonholes* ("Dynamite"), *Snarl* ("Gold Stars"), *South Florida Poetry Journal* ("Moon Over Moorhead"), *The Under Review* ("Eye of the Storm"), *Wigleaf* ("Judith in the Biblical Sense").

BRETT BIEBEL is the author of *48 Blitz* (2020) and *Winter Dance Party* (2023). His short fiction has been anthologized in *Best Small Fictions* and *Best Microfiction* and featured in *Wigleaf*'s Top 50 Very Short Stories. He teaches writing and literature at Augustana College in Rock Island, Illinois.